It Was a
Pretty
Good Year

Also by
JANE FLORY

It Was a Pretty Good Year

JANE FLORY

HOUGHTON MIFFLIN COMPANY BOSTON 1977

Library of Congress Cataloging in Publication Data

Flory, Jane, 1917-
It was a pretty good year.

SUMMARY: Portrays life in the early 1900's through the adventures of a young boy and his family.

[1. Philadelphia — Fiction. 2. Family life — Fiction]
I. Title.
PZ7.F665It   [Fic]   77-21782
ISBN 0-395-25835-9

For Barney, who remembered it all.

1

Barney was ten years old, and ten was just the right age to appreciate the joys of Reed Street — the sounds, the sights, the smells.

There was the noise, the constant noise. Clattering of horses' hoofs on the stone street that ran between the rows of tightly packed brick houses. Clattering of shoes on the brick sidewalks. Someone's mother was always yelling for somebody to go in or go out and not to hold the door open. Somebody's father was always calling to a neighbor up the street or over the back fence.

1

The butcher bellowed when he drove slowly up the alley. The huckster yelled, the iceman yelled, the horseradish man yelled. There was a fish man twice a week, the strawberry man in season, and the umbrella mender and the knife grinder. All of them called out that they were on their way. Only the milkman and the breadman made their deliveries early in the morning without a shout, but the hoofs of their horses clumped in the early gray dawn.

Often Reed Street echoed with the thunder of dozens and dozens of steers being driven from the railroad siding to the slaughterhouse on Washington Avenue. Steers from wall to wall, right up on the sidewalk, herded by drovers with long sticks who tried to prod them off the steps.

The steers made Mom furious. "Those wild cows!" she said. "Running by here like a wild west show! Innocent little children in danger — get in here, Barney, you know what I said — not speaking about the mess they make, and the smell, ugh!"

The innocent little children were out on the steps anyway, regardless of what their mothers were shouting, but they kept the front door open just in case a wild cow plunged up the front steps. The steers mooed and bellowed and ran, and when it was all over, Barney and Rob and Morris, and Benjie, too, if he could be found, took buckets and sluiced off the sidewalk and street. Mom said if she wanted her house to smell like a cowshed she'd live in a cowshed, and no back-talk, start sweeping. All up and down Reed Street the children were sweeping and dumping buckets of water and holding their noses. They didn't mind that much. It made them part of the cattle drive.

Barney complained that cowboys didn't have to clean up after the cows, and Mom said, "So go west, then, if you want such an easy life. Here in Philadelphia you scrub. Another pail of water, there, Rob. I want you should do a good clean job."

There were plenty of good smells too on Reed Street. Knockwurst and sauerkraut from the Schermerdines' and the O'Rileys' bubbling stew. Mrs. Finneran boiled cabbage endlessly, and her house reeked of it, but out on Reed Street it smelled fine. There was usually a chicken or two stewing at the Freedmans', and you could feel full just passing the Vitalli house. Garlic and cheese and rich sauce. Good.

In the summer there was the fragrance of sweet corn in the steamer on the corner in front of Kleinhoffer's Saloon. The man came with a little wagon full of corn and a great bubbling kettle. You could smell it for a block away. Two cents an ear, and a brush to lather on all the butter you wanted.

3

In the winter, the roasting chestnuts perfumed the air, and kept your hands warm, too, if you had a nickel for a bag of them.

Over everything else, all year round, floated the essence of heaven — fresh bread baking at Kolb's bakery behind Reed Street. Cinnamon buns and doughnuts and cupcakes. If you got lost somehow in the busy bustle of South Philadelphia in 1910, you could follow your nose to Reed Street, day or night, picking up the sweet smell of Kolb's bakery like a homing pigeon. You could find your way home.

Reed Street had everything. Music when the hurdy-gurdy man came around and cranked out his tunes. The monkey with his wrinkled little-old-man's face bowed and held out his hat when the music was over. They took turns dropping in the penny each week, first Ida because she was the oldest, then Adella, and right down the line, with always an argument about whose turn it had been last week.

There was more music in the summer evenings when the German band came around to play in front of Kleinhoffer's Saloon. First the players had a mug of frothy beer all around to wet their whistles, and then the concert. They were mostly stout men, portly figures in their red uniforms with gold braid on epaulets and sleeves, big mustaches and powerful lungs.

The parents and the girls sat on the steps to listen

and fan, but the boys crowded around, jumping back as the swinging doors opened and closed. Sometimes a contented customer handed over a pretzel as he passed. They divided it as evenly as they could and then sucked on it slowly. With luck, a small piece would last until the next pretzel came their way.

Mom didn't like that. "Hanging around a saloon, waiting for a handout. I don't like it." But Pop laughed.

"No harm done. They aren't going inside, just standing and listening. There's no boy on earth who could close his ears to that oom-pah-pah."

The big girls on Reed Street sat sedately on the steps spreading their full muslin skirts so the embroidery showed. While the light lasted the little girls played hopscotch, but as the shadows grew longer and deeper, they too stopped their activity. It was enough to sit and drink lemonade and listen to the steady stream of marches and polkas and waltzes that blared from the great brass horns. The bass drum pounded its steady beat, as if it were the heart of Reed Street.

The customers of Kleinhoffer's Saloon dropped coins in the little pail by the feet of the band leader, and that was music of a kind, too, a gentle tinkling under the heavy booming.

Sometimes Barney thought he was the only one in the family who really enjoyed every minute of Reed

5

Street, all year long, from morning until night. Pop and Mom, too hard-worked, stopped to enjoy Reed Street only once in a while. At four, Isaac was too young to have much freedom, and Rob, who was six, was restricted to just the block between Ninth and Tenth. Morris was the studious one who lived most of his life in books, and Benjie at thirteen ranged far beyond Reed in all directions. Adella was fourteen and Ida was fifteen, and they were both endlessly busy with school and housework and fixing their hair and practicing the piano and worrying about boys and learning to knit. Even Sport, their little pug dog, was too old now to run with the big boys. He spent most of his time snoring and snuffling on Isaac's cot. Only Barney, of all the Freedmans, could enjoy to the very hilt the delights of Reed Street.

He was sure he was the only one who really understood the magic of the acrobats. You never knew about the acrobats. You never knew just when they'd come. Sometimes often, sometimes not for weeks, but the stir of excitement was always the same. There was a minor wailing of some kind of wooden flute and rhythmic rattling on a little drum, enough to warn anyone who was inside to get out and settle down on the steps in time for the act. They usually came after the sun was really down, after the last light had gone out of the sky and the

6

haze of July heat was like a violet fog. Then the costumes looked like heavy ancient silks and the sequins were real jewels that flashed in the glow from the torches.

Whole families were out on the steps, talking and laughing and fanning with the paper fans from Dagney's Funeral Parlor. Sometimes Pop had a beer, but usually they all drank lemonade. Once in a while they had a strawberry spritzer, strawberry syrup with a spritz of carbonated water to make it fizzy. A small piece of ice was enough to cool the whole pitcher. Nobody on Reed Street wasted ice.

When they heard the flute, they stopped talking. It was not a time for conversation.

They carried everything with them, those Yugoslav acrobats. Like magicians from out of nowhere they unfolded two metal stands and thrust their smoky torches into them. Like a flash, four of them unfolded a carpet, patterned with flowers like an oriental garden and thickly padded underneath to cover the rough street and make a firm, flat surface for their tricks.

Maybe the acrobats were not beautiful. Mom said they were a greasy lot. Maybe seeing them by the full light of day Barney might have noticed that the head of the troupe, who seemed to be the father, was losing his lithe swiftness, that he panted after the tower of all nine of them leaped down to bow.

7

Maybe the plumpish woman who was probably his wife was not as young as she seemed by torchlight, and if you cared to look closely, her tight green satin blouse showed a roll of fat around her waist. But the young ones, four sons and three daughters, were like young princes and princesses, enchanted, enchanting. There was a girl, not too much older than Barney, maybe eleven or twelve, and when they finished their act and packed up, Barney longed to take the girl's hand and follow wherever the acrobats went, be it halfway around the world.

They spun and tumbled and leaped up light as windblown feathers to land laughing in a pyramid on each other's shoulders. When the papa of the troupe said "hup" they leaped to the ground and bowed.

Once when they came, a new man was with them. He hurled himself high into the air, tumbling to the sound of the drum he himself was playing, over and over and over in space, and then back on his feet, bouncing lightly on his toes. Still playing the drum.

That night when the velvet fez was passed around, Pop dropped in two dimes. Mom gasped and frowned at him.

"Is it a millionaire you've gotten to be —" she began, but Pop smiled dreamily.

"To turn over and over in the air like that, never to miss a beat, to tumble and drum, too — Besides, it was a good day today. Mrs. Kuhneman ordered three new dresses.''

Mom said severely, "Still, five cents would have done.''

"Esther, to jump like that, drumming, even five dollars would not be too much.''

The show was over, and the torches were gone. Barney put his hand in Pop's and they all went in to bed.

2

It wasn't easy, growing up in a family like Barney's. There were the two girls, such nice girls, everybody said. Pretty and polite and good in school. It was hard to live up to the example they set. Then came Benjie, who was not pretty or polite or good in school. Benjie was strong and clever and adventurous and BAD. If there was trouble, Benjie had thought it up and was leading the action. Benjie had figured out a way to make his world run on his terms. Mom and Pop had no doubt that Benjie would rise to the top.

"But to the top of what?" Mom worried. "The cleverest boy in Reform School maybe?"

It was certainly not easy to live in Benjie's shadow, with teachers expecting the worst of you in school, and friends expecting another kind of worst, a fine dashing kind of worst.

Then came Morris, who was so bright it hurt Barney's head to think about it. He was the brightest kid that ever hit the James Wilson Elementary School, and when Barney stumbled along only one year later every single teacher thought he would be as bookish as Morris or else as bad as Benjie. When all he wanted to be was Barney.

And now to top it off, both Benjie and Morris had announced what they intended to do in life. For the rest of their *entire years*, at thirteen and eleven, they *knew*! The bombshell dropped one night at supper, and even Pop and Mom were impressed.

"Have some more herring, you should grow up strong and healthy," Mom had said.

"I don't have to be strong and healthy," Morris objected. He didn't like herring much. "I'm going to be a college professor, so I don't have to be healthy."

"A professor!" Pop was amazed. "For that you have to go to college first."

"There are scholarships," Morris explained. Under cover of the conversation Barney slipped the

11

herring from Morris' plate. No need to waste good herring just because years from now Morris was going to college.

"A scholarship is if you study hard they let you go to college for not so much money," Morris explained to Mom, who had clutched her heart. "Maybe for not any money at all. So all I have to do is study hard and get a scholarship." He beamed at his parents from behind his thick glasses. "Now that I know what I am going to be, it'll be easy."

Benjie nodded. "I'm going into business for myself someday. I've got it all figured out."

"Oho, my boy! For a business for yourself you got to pay attention in school and learn your figures well. No spitballs when you got your own business, no tossing erasers out the window, no — what was it last week? — sneaking out of class to play ball."

Benjie shook his head. "I got that planned out too. I don't have to be good at arithmetic, all I have to do is hire someone who is. It's easy."

"*President* of the Reform School, he'll be," Mom murmured.

Barney chewed on the herring in awed silence. It had always been understood that Ida and Adella would marry nice young men and keep clean houses and food on the table every bit as good as Mom's.

Now Benjie and Morris had decided their futures. That meant that Barney was next.

"When did you make up your mind, Morris?" he asked finally.

Morris looked up from his second helping of creamed potatoes. "On my birthday. When I turned eleven I decided I'd better make up my mind."

Eleven! There was no time to lose. Less than a year to decide what he would be. Of all the choices in the world, which would he, Barnett Freedman, take? It was a terrible responsibility.

On Saturday Pop got a hot lunch. The rest of the week he carried his lunch from home in the morning, meat loaf sandwiches or whatever was left over from the weekend roast. But on Saturday, with the children home from school, they took turns carrying him a basket with a towel-wrapped casserole of stew or a container of soup with whatever treats Mom tucked in around the sides to hold it steady.

Isaac and Rob were too little to go so far, Ida and Adella were taking their music lessons, but Benjie and Morris and Barney were supposed to take turns. Benjie lived a life of his own, complicated by games that were scheduled to begin promptly at nine at Kolb's lot, or friends he had to meet at the corner of Tenth and Reed. Morris always had books due at the library, and if he didn't return them, he'd have to pay a fine.

Barney was free. He and his best friend, Charley Schermerdine said "see you" when they parted the day before, and they always did, but they drifted together, no special time, with the understanding that either Mrs. Freedman or Mrs. Schermerdine might interfere with plans of her own.

The trip to Pop's tailor shop at Eleventh and Locust was not one of the chores Barney objected to, really. Outside he did. He said, because he felt it was expected of him, "Why can't Benjie? Why does Morris always have to go to the library? Why always me?" But truthfully he was glad that his turn came much oftener than once in three. It was an adventure into a different world. Barney was all for adventure, in whatever form it took.

Once in a while he asked Charley if he wanted to come along. Charley always did, but often as not he had to scrub the already snow-white front steps. Barney really preferred to go alone. It was less complicated. Still, if Charley could get started on the steps early enough, and Barney helped, they could have an early lunch and go off together.

There were worlds out there beyond Reed Street. As wonderful as it was, Reed Street was only part of the spinning universe, and Barney longed to see it all. There was time for the Saturday chores and a quick game of peggie and lunch, and by eleven-thirty the basket was ready, covered with a checked dish towel. Barney set off to the world beyond.

The nine hundred block of Reed Street was a mixed bag of nationalities, and none of those took their ethnic background too seriously. The Schermerdines thought of themselves as German-Americans, and Mr. Schermerdine sang with the German Chorale Society. They went to the Lutheran church three blocks away and they truly didn't care that the Freedmans went to synagogue only on High Holy Days, and then mostly because Aunt Dora-by-marriage felt very strongly about synagogue attendance. The Connellys and the O'Rileys went to Mass every morning as a matter of course, and the Finnerans only on Sunday. But all the ladies visited across the fence when they had a minute on wash days, and Mom had more ideas in common with Mrs. Connelly than with her own sister-in-law, Dora. So they went their neighborly ways and sent around chicken soup and stew and blood pudding sausage when someone was sick, and one was as good a cure as the other.

Anyone could walk down that area of Reed Street without a challenge. It was a public street, free to anyone who didn't come prepared to make trouble.

15

Bloody feuds were settled on Kolb's lot, anyway. The Catherine Street section was another matter. The Italian boys owned every bit of it and would not give up a single inch without a struggle. And the way to Pop's shop led through it. It was possible to go a few blocks farther around and avoid it altogether, but that never occurred to Barney. The challenge belonged to Saturday, and Barney rose to meet it.

This particular day Barney had invited Charley to go along. Charley was an only child, so all the chores that were divided in the Freedman household fell on him. At last he was finished, front steps scrubbed, coal bucket full, ashes out, a quick trip to the corner store for things Mrs. Schermerdine had run out of, and at last his mother said, "Now you may go. Watch when you cross the street — those big brewery horses — and don't speak to any strangers."

Mrs. Schermerdine was a timid little woman. She feared a lot of things, but most of all she worried that Charley would be run over by a team of the great Percheron or Clydesdale horses that pulled the brewery wagons. If she had known of only half the dangers that Charley met and faced in Barney's company, she would have locked him in his room. But she didn't, so on special Saturdays he was allowed to go with Barney to carry the lunch basket.

16

It seemed a respectable errand, safe enough if it was neither too hot nor too cold, too windy nor too wet.

"It really is safe, isn't it? Except for those five blocks, and we got good legs," Charley said.

"They've never caught me yet," Barney boasted. "But leave your penknife at home, just in case."

"Would they take the lunch?"

"No!" Barney was shocked. "They're mean, but they aren't wicked!"

Rob and Barney had spent the earlier part of the morning kneeling on the grating in front of Kolb's bakery, probing with a broomstick for pennies. It was hard on the knees, but worth it, for this morning the wad of chewing gum on the end of a stick had brought up three pennies, a nickel that they put in the savings jar toward a BB gun, and a slug that might possibly be used on the trolley someday when there was a crowd.

The people who paused in front of Kolb's window to gaze in awe at the huge machines kneading the bread were a careless bunch, it seemed. How could anyone let a nickel fall and not make any effort to retrieve it.

"They must blow their noses a lot," reasoned Rob, "and the money comes out with their handkerchiefs. I'd use my sleeve."

Once a coin had fallen through the grating it was

lost forever, except to small boys with the patience to wield their broomsticks and fish around four feet below for anything shiny.

On this particular day they decided to give the third penny to Charley. It was a lot, but he was kept so busy at home that he rarely had time to work the grating. After the lunch basket was delivered Barney and Charley could shop at their leisure in the center city. Rob and Sport had an appointment out on the lot behind Kolb's to fight another first-grader. The challenge had been issued on Thursday. Already Rob had forgotten what they had quarreled about, but the fight would be a good one anyway. And it was time that Rob learned to take care of himself. Barney wondered for a moment if Smelly Huggins would be hanging around, the big bully. Then he dismissed Smelly from his mind as Mom came out with the basket.

"Hold steady, don't lash it around," cautioned Mom. "Walk slow and easy. The stew shouldn't spill over, but don't walk so slow it should get cold. Your Pop likes his stew hot, even on a warm day like this."

Barney promised, anxious to get on his way. Sometimes it seemed between Mom and Mrs. Schermerdine they'd never get going. The promises were given with the fingers of his left hand crossed behind his back so they didn't count as lies. There was no way that he could walk slow and steady all the way, but Mom didn't have to know that.

The dangerous part was the five-block walk between Washington and Bainbridge. The Italian boys lay in wait to chase outsiders passing through, shouting, "Shell out! Shell out!" If you could outrun them, fine, no hard feelings. But if you were caught and surrounded you had to shell out the contents of your pockets — jackknife, marbles, pennies, whatever you might be carrying.

First they walked quickly but normally, trying to look as if they belonged in the neighborhood. Often it worked. Today was one of those days it didn't. The boys were out in force this morning, yelling "Shell out!" as soon as they noticed Barney and Charley. Barney had prudently left his knife at home, but there were the pennies to protect. He was a good runner; the problem was the lunch basket. It had to be held on an even keel so the stew would not spill over into everything else. Barney had worked out a strange walk-run, it was neither one nor the other, that covered the ground quickly yet smoothly, while Charley pounded along at his side.

"Here we go," said Barney, "It's only five blocks."

The first two blocks were fine, but after that they

began to be winded. Some of the boys following them lost interest and dropped out, but four still chased along shouting, "Shell out! Shell out!"

Barney had kept Charley's penny in his pocket, intending to present it later as a big surprise. He was determined that their hard-earned wealth would not be taken away from them.

"It's not fair," panted Charley. "We — let any-body — walk on Reed — Street —"

"Shut up and run!"

Charley obeyed, but in a minute said, "My — marbles are holding — me back!"

Marbles! Charley had forgotten to leave his bag of marbles at home. It would take him months to win back all those good aggies and cat's eyes.

Barney grabbed Charley's hand and dragged his friend after him. The unwritten law said that after Bainbridge Street they were safe, but that was a block away. Alone, Barney thought, he could make it, but with Charley?

A grocery wagon clattered past and stopped a few doors down the street. For only an instant it blocked the view. As if there had been a plan, an uncovered trash can stood by a cellar door.

Barney put down the basket, grabbed Charley by the seat of the pants and toppled him head-over-tincup into the can, popped on the lid, then crouched behind it himself, holding the precious lunch basket cradled in his arms. He dared not look out, but he could hear the greengrocer arguing with a housewife, then cursing the four boys who came plunging into him just as he was weighing out spinach. When the horses started out again, the boys had been turned back by the indignant housewife, who screamed at their retreating backs.

Barney waited a while longer just to be sure it was safe. He could hear Charley panting inside the can, and behind it he too was catching his breath. When the street was empty again, he helped Charley out and brushed him off. Then the rest of the trip was made in dignified triumph.

When they arrived at the shop, Pop said, "Charley, you're all dusty. You fell down, huh?"

Charley launched into an explanation, but Barney nudged him vigorously to shut up. Since Charley did not have older brothers to explain the ways of life to him, Barney tried to pass on what Benjie and Morris had taught him. The main thing was that you never explained to grownups more than you thought was good for them to know.

Pop got out a clothes brush and brushed Charley's coat, and one-two-three, so fast they couldn't believe, sewed on a hanging button.

Pop looked at the neat lunch basket and beamed.

"Right on time. That's my good boys. You want to stay around for a while and visit, or you got business?"

It was a nice shop. Pop did fancy tailoring — ladies' suits and coats for the fashionables who lived on Locust Street. There was a half-finished coat on a figure, ready for braid and buttons, and in the back room a pile of cloth ready to cut out and sew. It was always interesting there, but they had other things to attend to.

"We got business, Pop," said Barney, and so they went on their way.

There was a store nearby that sold magic tricks and practical jokes. "Take your pick, Charley," said Barney grandly as he handed his friend the penny. "It's all yours. Spend it any way you want."

It was a fine moment. Charley was goggle-eyed with surprise and delight. "The cootie box is a good buy for the money," added Barney.

It was an event to savor for a long time. Maybe he would turn out to be a man like Mr. Andrew Carnegie and give away hundreds of dollars. He thought that idea over and then discarded it. A penny here and there, maybe. That felt good. But a hundred dollars would hurt.

3

They were always driven by the need for money. Pop made a living, but just barely, and with seven children to feed and clothe there was never anything left over. If Pop had heard about allowances, he would have laughed. If you needed money, no one handed it out to you just because you happened to be a member of the family. Music lessons, yes, provided you showed some interest and practiced faithfully every day without prompting. But an allowance? For what? For being alive and breathing? Money was to earn.

An event like the circus was something the Freedman children worked and saved for, for weeks and even months. September was not a bit too early to start saving. After a council meeting, at which Benjie did most of the deciding, the boys decided that since they would probably be forbidden to own a BB gun anyway, the few coins in the jar would be split evenly between them, and they could concentrate on saving for the circus.

Forget the admission fee; that was out of the question. They would have to rely on sneaking in under the edge of the tent. There was the risk of getting caught by one of the circus policemen, but they had to take the chance. There were so many other things to pay for — the side shows and balloons and cotton candy. It would cost a fortune.

The circus wasn't due until spring, but earning the money wasn't something that could be put off until the last minute, and jobs were not easy to find. After all, almost every family had at least one boy to sweep the sidewalks and take out the ashes, and for spinsters like Miss Ferguson, Mom wouldn't allow them to accept a penny for the errands they ran for her.

"Poor thing, neither a chick nor a child, not even a nephew she hasn't got. Shame on you to think of it! If she offers you a raisin bun maybe, something like that you can take, but money — never!"

Mr. Kleinhoffer swept the sidewalk in front of the saloon himself. He said he liked to get out in the sunshine once in a while. But he didn't like to shovel snow. Since his was a neighborhood business he tried to be fair about the boy who got the chance to shovel. When it came to Barney's turn, spring seemed so far away that he rashly spent the money on a magnificent pocket knife and a licorice cigar. The magnificent knife had blades that would not hold an edge and broke easily, so he had to go back to his faithful old knife. The licorice cigar was long gone and not even a dreamy memory of its deliciousness remained.

Benjie said, "You gotta learn sometime, kid. Better now than later." It was easy for Benjie to be philosophical when it was not his money that had been wasted.

Barney worked occasionally helping the Dutch bakers at Kolb's ice cupcakes. They dipped into the icing bowls — pink, white, chocolate — with their hands and with one expert sweep iced the cupcake and finished up with a little swirl. The neighborhood boys squeezed through the basement windows and were never turned away by the jolly Dutchmen, and never told to wash their hands first, either. They were paid in cupcakes, as many as they could eat. It made for a wonderful stuffed feeling, but no money.

Very early one morning, so early that it was still

black as night, Barney awakened. The bedroom he shared with Morris and Rob was at the back of the house, and he couldn't hear a sound on Reed Street. But on Tenth he could hear the wheels of Kolb's bakery wagon rumbling over the paving stones and the sound of the horses' hoofs, muffled by their clumsy rubber silencers, thumping along. No one else in the world was awake.

It was at that moment that the idea struck him. As quickly as he dared he crept out of bed, fumbled for his pants and jerked them on right over his nightshirt. Somewhere on the chair there should be his jacket and stockings — here were his shoes, and he was out the back window as silently as a thief. The window had been well greased, for this way out was often used when it was necessary to make a hurried exit. Out on the shed roof, then down the drainpipe, and that was easy enough. Out the back gate and down the alley and along Tenth to catch up to the baker's wagon.

Mr. Obendorf was never surprised at anything, not even at the sight of Barney dashing out of the darkness with his uncombed curls standing up all over his head and his nightshirt tail flapping.

"Do you need a helper, Mr. Obendorf? Somebody to deliver the orders?"

Mr. Obendorf was a slow, deliberate man. He thought a long moment while he stroked his straggly mustache. The horses whinnied softly and stamped. They knew it was time to move on. Barney was still panting from his dash down the alley.

"Could be I might use a smart boy to help me. Gets tiresome climbing on and off the seat at every house. You smart, Barney? Can you learn quick? Dumb I can get plenty of."

"Oh, I'm smart as a whip. Just try me."

"We could try. Hop up here, then, and climb over into the back. And listen careful, now, I don't chew my tobacco twice. Take the basket. Two plain loaves and a dozen cinnamon buns for the Hagertys and three Pandandies for the Joneses and one Pandandy and six cupcakes for the O'Mearas. And don't make a sound."

Hands trembling, Barney did as he was told, trying desperately to remember which order went to each house. He put the breads on the front steps beside the bottles of milk that had already been delivered. Then he came back to Mr. Obendorf for more orders.

"Just this once I'll check you," the driver said. "Can't have no mistakes or I'll have a riot on my hands." Barney held his breath as Mr. Obendorf checked each doorstep.

"Exactly right. Not one wrong. You're hired, then, B.F., until you make a mistake. Dime a week and worth it. A load offa my feet."

So it went for five wonderful weeks. Rob and Morris never guessed, and Barney grew clever at leaving his shoes pointed so he could jump right into them and tie the laces when he was safely down in the back yard.

He got so good at the job that Mr. Obendorf didn't have to tell him what to take to each house, unless the order had been changed.

Once in a while a sleepy housewife raised her bedroom window and called out softly. "Leave an extra loaf, Mr. Obendorf, Harold's coming home for a visit." It was too dark and she was too sleepy to notice that the baker with the basket was short and mustacheless.

Sometimes the sun was already coming up when Barney crept back into the house. Going up the drainpipe was harder than sliding down, but as with the window they had long ago solved that problem by driving in a series of spikes alongside the pipe for hand- and foot-holds.

Once Rob woke up as he was sneaking back into bed.

"You go to the toilet a lot, Barney. You were gone when I woke up yesterday," he murmured drowsily.

"Hush, you'll wake up Morris. It's all the water I swallow when I brush my teeth." Satisfied, Rob turned over and was instantly asleep again.

As the days went by, his secret grew more dangerous. He knew what Pop and Mom would say. "When we think our children are safe in bed, they'd better be safe in bed. Enough!"

Once he heard Mom stirring in the kitchen as he came in. And, too, he needed that sleep. He fought off the drowsiness all morning in school and only recovered when they were released for recess and he could run in the fresh air and get wide awake again. Miss McGowen whacked his hands more than usual for inattention. Because he hadn't listened in class he had trouble with his homework. At last he knew it was time to say goodbye to Mr. Obendorf before Miss McGowen sent a note home to his parents.

But there it was, fifty cents! Five whole dimes! He had never been so rich in all his life. And neither had the big boys. For once, he had more money than either Benjie or Morris.

There had always been the problem of dogs. Their own pug, Sport, slept noisily at the foot of Isaac's cot all night. But most other dogs were out at night, being the watchdogs they were supposed to be. Usually they just barked from their own back yards, but on the night Barney had decided he would have to give notice, a huge dog was roaming loose, taking care of the whole neighborhood. He caught Barney by surprise just as he was bending to put an especially large order on a step. With a snarl, the dog leaped for Barney's seat but got only a piece of his pants. There was a rip, a rush of cold air, and Barney trampled the cinnamon buns he had just delivered in his rush to get away. Mr. Obendorf reached out a strong arm and dragged him into the wagon as the frustrated dog growled and snapped.

"Did he get you, Barney? Did he break the skin?"

Too scared to talk for a moment, Barney shook his head and then said, "Lucky these aren't my school pants. My Mom would be wild if I ruined them."

"I know," said Mr. Obendorf sympathetically. "Many's the time I've had my pants tore, and I've been serving this route for twenty years. My wife sewed a double seat in all my pants, just because that dog runs loose once in a while. If I had my way, I'd boot that critter from here to City Hall, but the Smiths are good customers and I don't dare. You sure you're not bit?"

Barney felt his behind cautiously. The seat of his pants was gone but the skin was unbroken. Suddenly he wasn't afraid any more, just angry. That blasted dog!

He grabbed a loaf of bread and leaped out of the wagon before Mr. Obendorf knew what he was about. He ran up the front steps and the big mongrel growled again and opened his mouth for another bite. Barney jammed the whole loaf into the dog's mouth with all the force of his strong little arms and his stronger anger. He grabbed up the missing piece of his pants and ran back to the wagon while the dog stood there, looking pop-eyed and foolish with the loaf of bread pushed halfway down his throat, unable even to growl.

Barney climbed into the wagon on his own this time. Mr. Obendorf was doubled over with laughter. They stood there a long time laughing together in the dim morning light until at last the horses grew restless and moved on.

"Have to charge you for that loaf, Barney," Mr. Obendorf said regretfully. "No, darn it, I'll pay for it out of my own pocket, that I will. I never laughed so hard for two cents wholesale in all my life!"

Barney scurried up the drainpipe when his route was finished. He had hated to tell Mr. Obendorf goodbye, but the time had come. He stuffed the torn pants in the back of the closet until he could find a time when Mom would assume he had torn them climbing a fence. His days as a regular working man were over, and in a way he was not sorry.

He squeezed into bed beside Rob for a few precious minutes of sleep before Mom called them. "One thing I know," he thought. "When I grow up I'm not going to deliver bread."

4

Morris came tearing home from the library one day early in October with his glasses all steamed up with perspiration. "There's a medicine show at Broad and Oregon on the vacant lot. A wagon and a magician and it's free! Hurry up!"

"You don't go a step until your homework is done," Mom said to Barney. "Morris had a perfect report card last month, but yours —!"

"Please, please," begged Barney. "I'll do it right after supper. I'll work all evening, all week, I promise. But the show'll be gone by tomorrow. Please,

Mom, I'll take out the ashes and not complain. I'll make our bed all by myself —"

"You'll die and the Irish saints'll carry you right up to heaven, you'll be so good," Mom said. "I know you, Barnett Freedman. But, all right, go anyway, if you'll take Rob. Don't let go of his hand for a minute. No, you take his hand, Morris. And be home in time for supper. Pop don't like to be kept waiting."

They were off before she could change her mind, dragging little Rob between them as they ran.

Medicine shows didn't come often, and any novelty was too good to pass up. Sometimes it was a Western with Indians dancing on the tailboard of the painted wagon and then standing stolid and expressionless as the medicine man extolled the merits of the wonderful mysterious tonic. It was always made of native roots and herbs known only to the Indians themselves — even he, the medicine man, was not trusted with the complete recipe that kept them so strong and muscular.

"Is it going to be Indians?" gasped Rob.

"No, it looked like a magician."

Even better, or at least as good. Entertainment was entertainment, and they were not choosy, as long as it was free.

Morris was right. This one was a magician. He was pulling a scrawny rabbit out of a silk hat as they

33

squeezed through the crowd and wormed their way to the front.

"I can't see," protested Rob, jammed in between his taller brothers. So they pushed him forward, shoving a little girl out of the way to get to the front row. She gave them a dirty look and dug Morris with her elbow, but his attention was on the magician, now pulling one colored scarf after another out of a tube that only a moment ago was clearly shown to be empty.

"Look closely now," he said. "Watch every move!" His hands flashed, and the scarves, crazy pink, purple, green, yellow, suddenly became an American flag that he waved triumphantly over his head. His wife, who handed him his props and clapped admiringly after every trick, wheezed out the "Star-Spangled Banner" on an accordion. They all stood at attention and held their hands over their hearts. It was an awesome moment. Barney felt a rush of patriotism and love of country — and then the flag was gone and the medicine man was wheeling a cart of bottles out onto the tailgate of the wagon that made his stage.

"You've been a kind and gracious audience," he said, beaming and bowing as his wife played "Pomp and Circumstance." Barney knew the tune because that was what old Miss Lippincott always banged out on the piano whenever something special was going on at school.

"Now I'd like to return the favor," continued the magician, "by showing you something that will help all of you, all of you, mind you. None are too old, none are too young — you there, sir, and you —" he pointed right at Rob. "Listen to what miracles this potion has produced. And every single miracle has been witnessed, signed and sealed by the grateful users." His wife waved a sheaf of papers, all decorated with official-looking red or gold seals and ribbons.

"We have here a young man — bring him on, my dear — who only a short time ago was thin, pale, wasting away. Doctors from all over did their best, but could find no cure. At long last his anguished parents came to me for help. Right out here, sonny, step carefully now." His wife led out a boy who seemed to be about thirteen or fourteen, a stocky specimen, blindfolded.

"He is blindfolded, for he is a fellow of tender sensibilities and would rather not admit publicly how weak and sickly he was so recently, so very, very recently. But you have my word, which is as good as my bond in any county of this and many other states of these great United States, that what I say is true. He lingered perilously close to death's door until his parents were advised as a last resort to try my Elixir.''

Morris and Rob and Barney stood transfixed. Near Death's Door! And now he certainly seemed to be sturdy enough, with a good broad chest and strong arms and legs.

"Turn around, my boy; show them your strong back, so recently hardly able to support you. My friends, this fine young man had to be carried from room to room so he could get a little sunshine through the windows, while his chums played outside and enjoyed all the boyhood pleasures he was missing. Flex your muscles, son, show them how active you are now, and every bit of it is due to the miracle-working powers of this wonderful Elixir!''

The boy did as he was told. He spun around with enthusiasm and made a fist and showed how his muscles bulged under his sweater. He waved his arms vigorously, and somehow the blindfold slipped!

The three Freedman boys crowded so close to the wagon gasped as they looked up at their brother Benjie! Benjie, who had never been sick a day in his life. Benjie, who could lick any boy his size for blocks around.

"Benjie! He's my brother!'' shouted Rob.

The medicine man leaped into action. "See, now he's returned to the bosom of his loving family, well and strong.'' He grabbed Benjie's hand and jumped off the wagon, hustling the four boys out of the crowd. "Back to your loving parents," he shouted, "and don't forget to keep on with your Elixir at the first sign of trouble."

"I guess you'll tell on me," said Benjie as they trudged home.

"Why did you do it?" Barney asked. "You knew it was all a lie."

"Because I got twenty-five cents," said Benjie sadly. "But if you tell, Pop'll wallop me and Mom'll make me take it back."

"Twenty-five cents! You got paid first?"

Benjie nodded. Barney thought it over. "The wagon'll be gone by the time we get home and tell and get back. So you couldn't give back the money. But you could share it and Pop wouldn't have to know."

"I think that's called blackmail," said Benjie.

"I think it's called you don't have much choice," said Barney wisely.

"Four into twenty-five is six and one quarter cents," figured Morris quickly. "If we make it four to Rob and seven to each of us big guys it works out better."

Big guys! Morris considered him one of the big guys!

Barney was no nearer the Great Decision of what he'd grow up to be, but surely he was making progress. Morris called him a big guy!

"How was the show?" asked Mom when they got home.

"Best we ever saw," said Morris enthusiastically.

"The magician was very good, and it had a sort of surprise ending," added Barney. Benjie looked glum and didn't say anything.

"Now eat plenty," said Mom, as she dished up the supper. "Chicken soup with matzoh balls. You're all growing boys and I want you should keep healthy and strong."

5

There were a few spindly trees on Reed Street, and they tended just to turn brown and dry in autumn. There was no blazing display of fall color. Even without it, there was no doubt that fall had arrived.

School had started more than a month ago and they were all settled in comfortably with their new teachers. Barney had a little trouble. Miss McGowen had taught Morris, and her first remark was that awful one that all new teachers made. "Another Freedman! How nice. I do hope you'll be as good a student as your brother Morris. Such a hard worker, a bright boy.''

Barney thought, ''She must have missed Benjie or she wouldn't be so lovey-dovey about the Freedmans.'' Oh well, what could you do? Last year, his teacher, Miss Lippincott, had had Morris, too. Each teacher tried hard, but after a while each one in turn had to realize that Barney was not Morris, nor did he intend to be. When that was established, Barney and his teachers got along tolerably well.

The beginning of school marked the end of summer, but summer weather often lingered well into October. They itched and scratched in their school suits and black stockings and sighed with relief when the heat went out of the brick sidewalks and the air began to feel crisp and bracing.

Then Miss McGowen brought out the pumpkin patterns and the whole class traced pumpkin faces onto manila paper and colored them orange. The pattern slipped somehow as Barney drew around it, and his pumpkin ended up with a cock-eyed leer. He considered asking for another piece of paper and doing it again, and then decided against it. One of the twenty-eight pumpkins could have a slightly evil grin. He colored it as bright an orange as he could get out of his stump of crayon. Miss McGowen looked at it and sighed, but she hung it in the window with the rest of the pumpkins. Twenty-seven were smiling pleasantly, and one looked as if he were planning something delightfully wicked.

Halloween was celebrated with enthusiasm on Reed Street and the blocks nearby. There was the mischief that would have grounds for severe punishment at any other time, but under cover of the holiday and darkness and disguises, it became all right. And then there was the candy they collected. Not a lot, but more than they ever had at any other time of the year.

Henry Curtis had a store-bought Halloween costume, a pirate suit, but he had worn it for at least three years, with the shirt getting tighter and the pants shorter. Everyone else wore whatever came to hand, whatever changed their appearance and hid their true evil character and intentions.

The closet under the stairs to the second floor was a treasure chest. Mom could never bring herself to throw away a garment, even when it had long outlived its usefulness. So besides the coats that hung neatly on hangers there was a big box in the back where the stairs sloped down, full of great stuff. There were long full skirts and fitted jackets, and a dress or two with the bustles that no one had worn for years and years. And hats! Little bits of flowers and feather-covered felt and great broad-brimmed straws that Ida and Adella had worn until no amount of refurbishing would make them do.

Even Benjie, grown up as he was, got in the spirit of Halloween. He would dress up, but he wouldn't stoop to rummaging through the closet with the little kids to find a special outfit.

"Just toss me out anything," he said gruffly to Barney, who was pawing in the inky darkness under the stairs. "No, not that, for gosh sakes, can't you find anything decent, bonehead?"

A long navy skirt came flying out and one black glove.

"Criminy!" he shouted. "What kind of idiot do you take me for? I got a moron for a brother!"

"Hush!" Mom yelled from the kitchen. "You're all cut from the same piece of cloth, so no calling names. If one's a moron, you're all morons, and Pop and I got no moron children, so no more already!"

Barney's remarks were muffled. "I can't see in here and I can't hear and you keep complaining. Darn it, you don't like what I pick out, you do it yourself."

Benjie shut up then and took whatever was tossed to him. Then Morris chose an old suit of Pop's with rubber bands around the ankles to keep the legs from dragging. Rob giggled as Ida buttoned him into a dress she and Adella had outgrown. Isaac had a long nightgown that Aunt Dora had sent over in a bundle of hand-me-downs.

They all hustled off to the kitchen to have Mom

blacken their faces with cork. She always supervised this. "Otherwise you'd burn up every good cork I've got and set fire to your hair besides."

Still in the closet, Barney couldn't make up his mind. If only he could see better. He had an idea he had helped his brothers to the best of the lot, but it was too dark to be sure.

The dining room was just through the doorway, and in a second he was searching in the sideboard for a candle. No need to light a new one, a short burned-down one would do. The matches were right there in the drawer, too. Mom kept a neat house with everything in its place.

With his little candle lighting the darkness, Barney could see fine. He quickly grabbed up a broad-brimmed hat trimmed with squashed roses, a long sweeping skirt and a feather boa that was three yards long and had lost most of its ostrich feathers. Another hand-me-down from dear Aunt Dora. Did she think Mom or the girls would wear it? Like an endless skinny old squirrel's tail — a squirrel who had been through the wars. As he held up the blue boa and looked at it with distaste, Benjie called.

"Come on, half pint! Hurry up if you're going to come with us big kids!"

Barney wrapped the boa around his neck and hurried. He never gave the candle another thought until Mom was blackening his face. There was a pungent smell in the air that was — was it the burnt cork? No, something else was burning, and with a start he remembered the candle. He broke away while he was still only partly corked, and ran. A trickle of smoke was coming out around the edge of the closet door.

"Fire!" he yelled. "The closet's on fire!"

They fell all over themselves running to the hall-way, but over the noise they heard Mom yell, "Don't open that door! Wait, wait, I'm coming with water!"

Barney was there first and had already flung the door wide open. The sudden draft made the little smolder turn into a blaze. He hiked up his long skirt and began to stamp on it just as Mom arrived with the basin of water. She flung it into the closet right square at the back of his neck.

"More water! Bring more water!"

"It's out now, Mom," said Barney damply.

"More water anyway," cried Mom. "The whole house'll go next and we'll be on the street!"

Morris and Barney dragged all the remaining dress-up clothes out into the hall. "It's all out, Mom, not even a smolder."

Mom wasn't satisfied until every last coat was pulled off its hanger and examined.

"The fire's out," protested Barney. "Mom, we

gotta go! The rest of the bunch are hollering for us out front."

"Better them than the fire engine should be out front. Why, what's a candle doing here?"

This was what Barney had hoped to avoid. Mom had discovered the evidence and then the whole story came out. It was never possible to lie to Mom. She looked right through you, right down to the place where the lie started.

Luckily Pop was out in the back bringing in the garbage can and taking down the clothesline and wiring the back gate shut. He missed all the excitement, or Barney might not have gone out on Halloween at all. As it was, Mom sighed, "Barney, Barney, what will we ever do with you?" and let them go.

This was the first year the big boys had allowed Barney to go out with them. The O'Riley and Finneran girls and Ida and Adella were taking Rob and Isaac and the crew of young Vitallis to knock on doors and get candy on Reed Street. The big kids were heading for Passayunk Avenue and the stores before they finished up the evening by stealthily switching rockers from porch to porch, or cutting the clotheslines of anyone who had been dumb enough to leave their clotheslines out. And dumping garbage cans, and leaving notes in milk bottles that said "Please leave twelve quarts of whipping cream."

The first stop on Passayunk Avenue was Nunnemacher's Variety Store for masks. The big boys scorned the masks that covered the whole face, and in a way Barney was glad. Those clown and hobo masks had a peculiar smell of the cloth and glue they were pressed out of. The eye and nose holes were never in the right places and it was hard to breathe and even to see. Moving on to a black half-mask was a sign of growing up, and besides they cost only a penny.

When all nine of them, Benjie and his friends Joe and Lumpy Vitalli and Morris and his best friend Seymour Cohen and Henry Curtis and Phil O'Riley and Barney and Charley were outfitted, Mr. Nunnemacher gave each of them a nice bag of some kind of hard candy. They thanked him politely and waited until they were outside to check what was in the bags. Jelly beans. Jelly beans! Left over from last Easter and hard as rocks and all stuck together!

Mr. Nunnemacher never got rid of anything. If it didn't sell one year, he figured it would sell another, so wait awhile. He never put anything away, either. You could find Valentines in July or dusty Christmas ornaments in April. It was what Barney considered a *real* variety store, a fascinating warehouse of beat-up treasures.

They went from store to store along the avenue, picking up a small bag of loot at each place and munching candy corn as they went. They swung their long black stockings with the potato in the toe when they passed other groups, but the gesture only appeared threatening. No one was looking for a fight on Halloween.

"When do we do the mischief?" whispered Charley. The big boys hadn't wanted to let Charley come along.

"He's a Mama's baby," said Benjie. But Barney begged so hard they gave in. "You'll have to be responsible for him if trouble starts." Barney promised, but he hoped no trouble would start. He might have enough problems taking care of himself, the way Benjie and the others talked about it.

When they had covered both sides of Passayunk Avenue, Benjie said, "That's enough for that. Now we see what trouble we can stir up." Barney heard Charley suck in his breath, and try as he might he couldn't help shaking a little. Anything might happen.

They headed for Tenth Street. Those houses had porches, not just front steps, and here and there someone had foolishly left out a porch chair or a fern stand. Stifling their giggles, they crept up on the porches and exchanged chairs. They even unhooked a swing and carried it around to the back yard. Then they went to Ninth and Reed, along the alley that ran behind the houses in their block. They tried gates, opening them carefully so they wouldn't creak. Some, like the

47

Freedmans', were securely wired shut, but others were only locked, and it was simple to slide back the bolt. Some gates were easy to climb over, and this crowd was familiar with every fence for blocks around. Benjie, the leader, cut the clotheslines, but they all tipped over garbage cans and carried the lids into the next yard. Mrs. O'Riley had a line of diapers hanging out. Probably they weren't quite dry at dusk and then she must have forgotten about them. They distributed the diapers evenly up and down the alley, hanging one on each fence. Somehow it seemed terribly funny, stumbling around in the dark, hampered by their costumes and masks, trying so hard not to laugh that they almost choked.

It was Charley who remembered the best prize of all. The Huggins family on Ninth Street had never dismantled their privy when the street sewers were put in and bathrooms installed. It was seldom used, only when someone was working in the garden and was caught short. And they all disliked Smelly Huggins for the bully and cheat that he was. He was strong and mean and spoiled rotten besides. Smelly Huggins' privy was fair game.

"It's near the back," whispered Charley. "They've got a dog, but he knows me. My mama visits there a lot."

Morris clapped Charley on the back. "Good fellow, Charley. Lead the way."

The gate was securely closed, but scaling the fence was no problem at all if they left their bags and potato stockings in a heap in the alley. The yard was dark, but not pitch dark. Someone was in the kitchen, and by the light from the gas lamp they could see the privy.

"Over it goes," said Lumpy Vitalli. It was almost too funny to bear, and Barney found himself hiccupping because he tried so hard not to laugh.

Suddenly the back door opened and a man's voice said, "Get it over with, Prince. I'm not about to sit up all night while you — who's there? Is someone out there? Sic 'em, Prince!"

Prince came charging out. He didn't care about Charley's mama's friendship. He didn't remember Charley. He barked and snarled like a monster.

"Heave!" said Lumpy, and they gave the privy a heave that turned it over with a crash. Then they started over the fence.

Barney was the last one over the fence. Prince jumped for his long skirt and held on. There was a rip, the skirt tore off, and Barney was safe on the other side, running up the alley with the rest of the gang of big boys.

"What happened to your costume?" asked Pop as they sauntered in the front door a few minutes later.

"It got a little hot," said Barney. "I left it behind."

Benjie gave him an approving grin, and behind his glasses Morris winked.

49

6

The election night bonfires were over, and all that was left of the tremendous excitement were the memories and the singed paving blocks at the street crossings. The memories were good, though. Great heaps of scrap lumber, broken furniture, boxes, whatever would burn had been collected. All day on that November Tuesday the pile grew at the intersection of Ninth and Reed. Higher than Barney's head, then higher than Benjie's, then even higher than Pop's head. As soon as the polls closed at eight, it was lighted. Everyone, even Rob and little Isaac, was allowed to stay up and watch. It wasn't necessary to wait until the votes were counted. Everyone knew who would win. The same party had won in Philadelphia for as many years as anyone could remember. It was just a great big outburst of feeling and an excuse to do something that on any other night would have been against the law.

The flames crackled and soared as high as the rooftops. The neighbors on the four corners of Ninth and Reed watched with more than a little nervousness, for sudden gusts of wind could blow the flames sideways and bring them dangerously close to their houses. Once the paint on Kleinhoffer's Saloon got hot enough to bubble, but Mr. Dougherty, the committeeman of their ward, paid to have it repainted. So he won Mr. Kleinhoffer's gratitude and insured his vote for the next election.

Long after Mom made them all come in to bed, the firelight flickered and danced, but the boys in the back bedroom were not kept awake by it. After being out so late, they slept long and hard. And next morning when Barney went to school, there was only a pile of ashes that the street cleaners gathered up before he came back that way for lunch.

Then November stretched ahead, bleak and gray and cold. Yet in the cold there was always the promise of snow. They all watched the sky anxiously and tried to guess if the clouds were snow clouds or would bring only more rain.

One morning Barney woke up early. There was a different light in the room, a different sound filtering in from outside. He shivered at the window where the draft blew in around the old window frames. And there it was. Snow! It must have been snowing gently all night long and they didn't even know.

"Morris, Rob, get up! It's snowing!"

Morris mumbled and pulled the covers closer around him, but Rob was out of bed in a second.

"Oh boy, oh boy! Look at it, Barney, look at the way it's piled up on the shed roof!"

Oatmeal never tasted so good, and for once Mom didn't have to urge them to hurry, not to poke over their breakfast, to find their schoolbooks, to put on their rubbers. They were way ahead of her. Even the girls were excited. For once the girls could forget that they were almost young ladies and behave like children again. They would throw snowballs on their way to school too.

Miss McGowen had her hands full that day. She tried to keep the fifth grade's attention by discussing snow crystals and even opened the window and let some flakes fall on a piece of black cloth so they could study them under a magnifying glass.

Barney had been the most restless, so to keep him

quiet she gave him the honor of holding the glass while the others stared at the lovely six-sided crystals, all different. He tried to think about every one of those crystals, not one of them exactly like any other, but it was too hard. It was easier to think about hitching the sled to passing wagons and getting a free ride.

After school he raced home with his books and tossed them down in the vestibule. There was no time to waste on milk and cookies. Then out again into the snow that blew against his face and melted down inside his coat collar.

He had gotten only as far as Kleinhoffer's on the corner when the difficulty started. A dozen boys were there already, scooping up handfuls of snow and packing them hard into snowballs. There hadn't even been time to choose up sides and start a proper fight. They were waiting until everybody got there.

Barney and Lumpy Vitalli were making their first snowballs and were getting ready to throw them when the door of the saloon swung open and Officer Hallahan came out, wiping foam off his mustache. He stepped right into a fast exchange of snowballs, not aimed at him at all. It was only chance that one of them hit him square on the side of the head, knocking his hat off.

He let out a bellow of rage, and before he had brushed the snow out of his ear and recovered his hat, the crowd had vanished around the corner. But Barney and Lumpy stood there a second too long, too surprised to move.

"Hah!" yelled Hallahan. "I've caught ye!" He grabbed Lumpy and shook him.

"He didn't do it," said Barney. "Lumpy didn't do a thing! That's not fair!"

Hallahan turned on him. "Argue with the Law, will ye? Assault an innercent victim, will ye?" He held Lumpy by the arm and grabbed Barney, too.

"I didn't do any assaulting either. You let go of me!"

Most of the policemen who patrolled the Reed Street area were big, friendly, fatherly men, and the kids rather liked them. But Officer Hallahan was disliked by everyone. He had a mean streak, and besides, he spent more time in the saloon than he did on the street.

Lumpy had set up a howl that brought Mr. Vitalli to the front door. Mr. Vitalli worked off and on, and this was one of his off times, so he was home in the afternoon. He hurried out in his shirtsleeves, struggling into his overcoat as he ran.

"What is it, Officer? What's the boy done?"

"Nothing," answered Barney. The Freedmans had all been taught to be respectful of the Law, but for the moment Barney forgot all he had been taught. Hallahan was wrong and had to be set right.

"Lumpy didn't do a thing and neither did I. We hadn't had a chance to get started —"

"Then you let go of them," ordered Mr. Vitalli. "Right's right, and if these kids didn't do anything, you go find the ones who did."

"Assaulting innercent victims and now back-talkin' the Law!" shouted Hallahan. He dragged the two boys toward the call box on the lamp post. He managed to control both of them with a strangle hold, while with one hand he fumbled for the key and unlocked the box. "Send the wagon to Ninth and Reed!" he roared. "Two criminals here, caught in the act."

Barney tried to mumble — "there was no act — didn't do it" — but the policeman paid no attention. Barney wished Mom would come out. She'd give Hallahan a piece of her mind, but their house was too far down the block, and she wouldn't have heard the commotion anyway, back in the kitchen. In no time at all the paddy wagon pulled up. The two dashing black horses and a black wagon. How many times Barney had stood awed as the Black Maria dashed by, carrying dangerous criminals to jail. And now he was one of those criminals.

The boys were hustled into the back of the wagon and ordered to sit still. "Then you'll have to take me too," said Mr. Vitalli. He climbed in and sat on the bench beside Barney and Lumpy. On the facing

55

bench another policeman eyed them stolidly, his hand on his night stick. He chewed tobacco steadily and just as steadily spit into the cuspidor in the corner. At another time Barney might have admired his perfect aim, but now he was too frightened to think about that.

Hallahan heaved himself into the front seat beside the driver, and they clanged off to the magistrate's office. By the time Officer Hallahan told his story, the crime had become considerably more dastardly.

"Deliberately aimed at and struck a woman bearin' a young child in her arms, yer honor, and broke a window to boot. Young thugs in the makin', sir, and they got to be disciplined."

"A woman with a child in her arms?" asked the magistrate, shocked. "Which one struck the blow?"

"Both," said Hallahan. "Both of them are guilty as sin, your honor!"

"What do you have to say for yourself" — the magistrate consulted the paper on which he had written their names and addresses — "Barnett Freedman?"

"I say Hallahan's lying," said Barney, scared, but more mad than scared. "There wasn't any woman or any broken window, only Hallahan got hit with a snowball, that's all, and me and Lumpy didn't even do that. Hallahan's a plain liar."

"Now there," said the magistrate sternly, "you've

got to be respectful. You can't call the Law names, no matter what you think."

"But he is a liar," insisted Barney stubbornly.

"And whatever happened, my boy had nothing to do with it, either," said Mr. Vitalli. "My committeeman is Mr. Dougherty, and he'll vouch for my family."

"Dougherty, eh?" The magistrate was thoughtful. Committeeman Dougherty took care of the area for blocks around Ninth and Reed, sent coal when a family was out of funds, a basket of food for the needy, a sympathy card when there was sickness or death. All in return for nothing at all but votes for his political party. He was a powerful man with City Hall, it was rumored. "Mr. Dougherty. Well."

The magistrate thought some more. "You can take your boy home, Mr. Vitalli. No case against him. And no case against Barnett. Just disrespect. You, Barnett, don't you see you can't go around accusing the officers of the Law? What would happen to our country if we let things go on like that, now? Wouldn't you like to take back your statement against Officer Hallahan?"

Barney shook his head. His voice shook, too, but he had the same stubborn streak in him that Pop did. "I can't. Hallahan's a liar, and that's the truth. I got to tell the truth."

"You can't defame a representative of the Law,"

insisted the magistrate. "It won't do. I'll have to send a notice to your father —" He waited expectantly for Barney to change his mind.

Barney's knees were as weak as water. He had big-mouthed himself into something serious if Pop had to be told. It would be so easy to say he guessed he had been mistaken, but he couldn't make the words come out. He shook his head and quavered, "Hallahan's a liar."

Officer Hallahan started to harangue, but the magistrate shut him up with a wave of his hand. "I'm in charge here, and don't forget it. I'm dispensing justice. You go home, Barnett Freedman, and your father will be notified. And you'd better not be brought up before me again or it'll go a lot harder with you the next time. You stay away from crime. Case dismissed." He closed his big book with a snap.

Barney dashed outside where Mr. Vitalli and Lumpy were anxiously waiting for him. "Don't worry, Barney," promised Mr. Vitalli. "Mr. Dougherty won't let you go to jail. I'll put in a good word for you."

Barney wasn't half as worried about jail as he was about Pop. What was he going to tell Pop?

It was growing dark as they trudged home. Mr. Vitalli, being out of work, couldn't spare the three nickels needed for the trolley ride. The snow was still falling gently, sparkling in the light of the gas lamps on the street corners. But it no longer held any charm for Barney. The trip to the magistrate's office in the paddy wagon had taken only a short time, but it was a long way home on foot. Mr. Vitalli had rushed out without a hat and he turned up his coat collar against the cold. Nobody had anything to say.

Mom started to scold the instant Barney came in the front door. "You know you're not supposed to stay out this late, Barnett! It's almost time for supper. Thank goodness you had sense enough to wrap up warm. Take off your wet stockings and get dried off. The very idea! The snow must have gone to your head."

"It went to Hallahan's head," thought Barney, but he didn't say it. At least if Mom was worrying only about wet feet it meant nobody had told. Nobody had let her know that her son, Esther Molly Freedman's son, had been hauled away in the Black Maria. At least there was something to be thankful for.

Benjie and Morris knew, but they made signs that their lips were sealed. Rob and Isaac had been playing with the other little kids out in the alley and probably hadn't heard about it.

All three older boys were unusually silent during supper, and Mom decided that they had worn themselves out throwing snowballs and were probably going to catch cold. She sent them all to bed early with hot bricks wrapped in old towels to keep their feet warm.

Benjie and Morris tried to get Barney aside to question him but Rob was always there. Besides, Barney didn't want to talk about it. It would all come out soon enough.

The next day Barney was so pale and big-eyed from lack of sleep that Mom felt his forehead and anxiously decided that he shouldn't go to school. He spent the day inside studying listlessly and finally taking a nap.

The next day the notice came.

It was there on the table in the parlor when Barney came home from school. Mom went in and looked at it curiously a good many times, but of course she did not open it. Barney went in a good many times, too, and each time the official-looking envelope seemed to grow bigger and bigger. He thought Pop would never come home to open it.

Finally he did. Supper was ready and on the table, but they all gathered around while Pop opened the letter. He read it through to himself once, then twice more. Then he said, ''The soup's getting cold, no, Esther? We'll eat, and then we'll talk about this.''

It was a strange supper. No one spoke, except to ask quietly for the salt or more bread. Even Rob and

Isaac knew that something was wrong. Only Sport chomped noisily on a bone in the kitchen.

Even before the table was cleared, Pop said, "Now, Barnett, tell me."

Barney told it from the very beginning. Pop's face was very stern as he sat in his armchair at the head of the table. Finally he said, "It says here I am to pay five dollars costs."

Five dollars! Mom gasped and clutched at her heart. It was a fortune. "Barnett —" she began, but Pop silenced her.

"There is only one thing important. I got only one thing to ask. Barney, my son, was Hallahan lying?"

Barney nodded.

"Then," said Pop, "I'll pay whatever it costs, even five dollars. You must always tell the truth, even if it costs. Now we won't talk about it any more. It is over."

He had told the truth and it had cost, but he had lived through it. Lumpy Vitalli was three years older and his father had come along to defend him. Barney had managed it all by himself.

And there was no getting around it, neither Benjie nor Morris had ever ridden in the Black Maria.

7

Barney was always coming home scraped and bruised, and often he dared not explain the reason to his mother. She deplored fights, but there didn't seem to be any way to stop them. Most of the street games they all played ended in free-for-alls no matter how peacefully they started. Other things were strictly forbidden for reasons that seemed perfectly understandable to Mom and made no sense at all to the boys.

The big boys, Benjie and his friends, spent a lot of time around the stable at Kolb's bakery. They talked to the grooms and the stable boys, patted the horses and occasionally were allowed to shovel piles of straw and manure. Mom forbade it. She said that characters who hung around stables were absolutely certain to go bad, to become gamblers or worse.

Barney, who was young enough to obey part of the time, looked forward to the time when he would be old enough to sneak over there any time he wanted instead of only once in a while.

One of the things the big boys did was to reach in cautiously and with a quick jerk pull out a hair from the horse's tail. The hair was strong and tangleproof and made a wonderful leader to fasten a fishing hook onto. Invisible in the water, it made the bait look as if it were swimming free, not attached to anything.

Barney fished with a slightly crooked willow pole, ordinary string and a bent pin, and seldom caught much. It may have been that there weren't many fish in the irrigation ditches and little stagnant ponds, but he felt sure that if only he had a leader he too could come home with a string of shiners like those that Benjie caught from the bank of Mingo Creek.

One morning he ducked Charley and went off to Kolb's by himself. He always felt uncomfortable when he was leading Charley astray. It was all he could do to cope with his own conscience, without turning Charley, too, into a Gambler or Worse.

Along with the big horses that pulled the bakery wagon, there were half a dozen pretty little ponies that were stabled there for the use of the Kolb children. The Kolbs lived in a grand house in the center of town. They had never been seen around the stable. When their ponies were wanted, a message was sent and several grooms hitched up the pony carts and drove them uptown.

Barney had never really seen a Kolb child riding in one of those little wicker carts, but he could imagine how stylish they must look. He didn't give them more than a passing thought, though. Their life was so far removed from his. Style just didn't enter into his life.

One day when he had carefully weighed his chances of going completely bad, and had decided it was worth the chance, he went over to the stables to watch the ponies. The big horses were gone most of the day, but some of the ponies were always there. On this particular day he was lucky. His favorite, a dappled gray, was there, chomping away at the food in his manger while a stable boy cleaned out the stall. The door to the stall was swung wide open, and the stable boy shoveled the dirty straw into a wheelbarrow and replaced it with sweet-smelling fresh straw.

"Don't you go foolin' around here, kid," the boy warned Barney. "These little fellows have a powerful kick. Run along now. Go on home and play on your own street."

He trundled the wheelbarrow off down the long barn to the manure pile out on the other side. Once he looked over his shoulder to see if Barney had obeyed him and could not see him, so he went out with his load. Barney intended to do as he was told, but found he couldn't. He just stepped behind a post where he could see his favorite. The dappled gray was short and strong looking and was spotted in beautiful dark and light spots. His name was painted on the stall, Starlight. That was a beautiful name for a beautiful little horse.

Suddenly Barney was overcome with such a strong desire for a hair from Starlight's tail that he forgot all the warnings. With a leader like that he would surely be able to catch bigger fish than Benjie and Morris and Joe and Lumpy had ever seen.

He stepped forward into the stall and ever so carefully selected one long silvery hair. Starlight looked over his shoulder and whinnied impatiently. He evidently didn't like strangers in his stall.

Barney heard the squeak of the wheelbarrow. The stable boy was coming back. He had to act quickly. He gave a strong jerk and the hair came out — and the next instant he was sprawled on his back. The stable boy came running.

"What did I tell you!" he shouted. "I said you'd get kicked! Are you hurt?"

Barney was too dazed to be sure. The boy looked him over.

"Your forehead's bleeding — where else did he get you?"

The breath was still knocked out of Barney and all he could do was to point to his chest. The boy pulled open his sweater and shirt and looked. "Just grazed you, I think. Six inches closer and he'd a knocked you straight into the next world. Now you go straight home, kid, and tell your mom exactly what happened so she can keep an eye on you in case you've got a broken head or a busted rib. If you start to puke or feel sleepy, that's bad!"

There was no way Barney could go home and explain to Mom exactly what happened. He had been forbidden to hang around the stable in the first place, and how could he explain why he needed a horse hair so badly? Still clutching the precious hair, he struggled to his feet and went slowly home. Mom was cleaning the parlor, so he went in the back door and up the stairs without being seen. He would just have to look out for himself.

A piece of ice would have felt good on the lump that was rising on his forehead, but to open the icebox door and chop off a piece would bring Mom down on him instantly. She had an instinct for the faintest sound around the icebox and would be there in a flash, calling, "Not the pudding! It's for supper! Keep out of the ice chest — you think ice grows on trees? You think the man delivers it free?"

When she saw his wounds she would be all sympathy, but after she had washed and bandaged him she would ask the inevitable question, "How does it happen you should come home cut and bruised?" And there would be nothing he dared tell her.

He spent the afternoon up in his room. At supper time Mom's eagle eye saw the bruises on his forehead. "Barney, you've been in trouble again!" He nodded. That certainly was true. He didn't have to lie about that.

"Who laid a hand on you? Who was it?"

"It — it was more like a foot."

"Oh my, you boys will drive me to an early grave with your soccer! No more soccer for you, you hear? And let me put some ice on that lump this minute."

He was so relieved that he had been spared the misery of either the truth or a lie that he allowed himself a little joke. "You think ice grows on trees, Mom? You think the man delivers it free?"

"Shut up your nonsense and let me tend to you. The idea, you could get your head smashed in, playing like that!"

He nodded. Mom was right. Righter than she

67

knew. His chest hurt, but he had a beautiful silver hair for a leader.

The bicycle wounds were something else again. There was no need to beat around the bush about how he acquired those. Mom knew from his yells of frustration and skinned knuckles just how the bicycle riding was going.

It happened this way. He had wished and longed and prayed and yearned for a bicycle, any bicycle, without one single shred of hope. There was no money in the family for a bike, new or used. It was hopelessly beyond his reach and Barney knew it, but that didn't keep him from wanting one. He even dreamed at night of riding, and woke Morris and Rob with his thrashing and churning.

Then he took Charley Schermerdine's advice and wished on a hay wagon. He did it just right, sighted the hay wagon, quickly turned his back and made his wish and went the other way. There was that awful urge to turn his head to see if the wagon was out of sight yet, but if it wasn't, the wish would *never* come true. It was no good if you told your wish, either, but Charley knew what it was going to be. He went through every bit of ritual correctly but with no conviction that it would really work. Still, it was like stepping on cracks. "Step on a crack, you'll break your mother's back." He had never heard of anyone's mother suffering because a careless child stepped on a crack in a cement sidewalk, but he never took chances.

He had almost forgotten the hay wagon when two days later he came upon his yearned-for treasure, waiting for him. It was uncanny. There it was on top of a trash barrel in the ten hundred block of Reed Street, waiting for him. Someone had thrown out a perfectly good bike in answer to his need.

Of course it wasn't *perfectly* good. It had been in a bad accident, no doubt about that. Bent almost double, spokes twisted, some missing, the rear wheel quite separate from the rest of the mechanism. But it was a bike, and that was enough to start on.

Barney and Charley hauled it down cellar and took a real inventory of what was missing. Some spokes — they could be improvised out of umbrella ribs — one pedal, not so easy, but a block of wood could be whittled to the right shape. Baling wire would hold the back wheel on.

It took a good part of his spare time that spring, fixing up the old bike. Mom hollered at him for being inside when he should be out playing in the sunshine. Then he would say innocently, "But you said I wasn't to play soccer, Mom."

"The boys were playing kick-the-can yesterday when I came home with the herring."

"That's even rougher."

"You never minded rough before —"

"Please, Mom, once it's finished I can ride outside in the sunshine and get twice as much sunshine because I can go twice as fast, see?"

Mom didn't see and was inclined to argue, but Barney had it all figured out. "Three times as much sun, even. The sun shines on Reed Street, right? I can ride all over Reed Street and get the sun. Then when I go across Ninth Street I get the Ninth Street sun, and the Tenth Street sun, which I can't do if I'm only playing kick-the-can on Reed Street."

Mom gave up. She felt there was something weak in his argument, but she didn't have time to put her finger on it. The rice pudding needed stirring.

Finally the bike was repaired. All he had to do was learn to ride it. He could have done that outside, but Benjie and Morris had laughed so hard at his old wreck. The whole O'Riley family had grinned, and Smelly Huggins hooted and hollered and made sure everyone noticed as he and Charley dragged it home. He couldn't face their laughter when he wobbled and fell off, as he was sure to do for a while. So he decided to learn down in the cellar.

The heater in the basement was a big monster with six or seven ducts going upstairs. It was like an enormous octopus. Barney had always been a little afraid of it and had dreaded the day when he would be old enough to have to go down to regulate the drafts as Benjie did. Now it became his friend.

The packed dirt floor was uneven, but not as uneven as the street would have been, and much softer. He rode from the coal bin to the heater to the water meter, round and round, reaching for support from the walls when he felt himself going down. Sport ran beside him, snuffling through his flat little pug nose and panting to keep up. The rough walls bruised and cut his hands, and his knuckles were always skinned. When he knew that the other boys were out he yelled, and that helped. But if any of them were around he clamped his lips together and didn't let out a sound. Ida and Adella sympathized, and Mom washed and bandaged his hands each evening.

"What makes you so stubborn, Barnett? You'll wear your hands out. Suppose you should want to play the violin, and no hands? If you'd ride outside, Benjie could hold up the bicycle until you've got the hang of it. I'll make him do it."

But Barney *was* stubborn. This was something he wanted to do alone. It seemed like forever, but really it was only a few days before he and Charley dragged the bike up the steps into the dining room and then out the front door.

The big boys watched respectfully as he made his grand appearance on the street. He was an immense

71

success. Not only did he ride without wobbling, but he rode his own bike. He soaked up the sun on Reed and Ninth and Tenth. Then before he ventured any farther he said to Charley, who was faithfully panting beside him, "Charley, now I'm going to teach you to ride. After all, the hay wagon was your idea."

8

Girls did not figure heavily in Barney's life. His own two sisters seemed almost to have joined the camp of the grownups. They were kind. Adella, especially, used to grab Barney once in a while and hug him, to his surprise and embarrassment. But Ida and Adella were pretty and clean and polite and punctual and good students. They practiced their piano lessons without urging. Ida's specialty was "Over the Waves." Pop called it "Over and Over and Over the Waves," because once Ida had memorized a piece and played it perfectly, she played it often. Adella was struggling with something Barney thought was oddly named "Rassles of Spring," but then, that was the trouble with grownups. So much that they did was odd, and they never bothered to explain.

Occasionally he had worshiped a schoolteacher from afar, but that never lasted long. As soon as the teacher discovered that he had very little interest in the nine times table, she began to be stricter and sharper, and Barney would wonder what he ever saw in her.

Then there was Edna Carroll, Willie's younger sister. Willie was in between Morris and Barney and good friends of both of them. The Carrolls lived over on Broad Street, which was much grander than Reed, but they weren't a bit stuck-up. Edna was in Barney's class and the prettiest girl he knew. She had yellow hair in shiny corkscrew curls and blue, blue eyes. The ribbon in her hair always matched her dress and was tied in a bow on top of her head. It looked like a huge butterfly that had lighted there for a moment. Her bows had a durability that other ribbons did not. Most girls went home in the afternoon with their hair ribbons drooping or even ink-stained. Edna was held in such high esteem that no boy seated in back of her had ever dipped her curls or her ribbon into the inkwell. Not even Smelly Huggins. That showed what kind of girl Edna was.

During the first week of June there was to be an

eclipse of the moon. The newspapers had written about it for days, and Miss McGowen took advantage of the event to make it a class project. She set up circles of cardboard that represented earth and moon and with the light from a magic lantern showed how the shadow of the earth would creep across the face of the moon and put it into darkness.

After school that day, as Barney was scuffling to be first out of the classroom, Edna Carroll stopped him.

"Barnett," she said shyly, "are you going to watch the eclipse?"

"You bet," he said. "I wouldn't miss it."

"Then would you like to watch it from my house? We have a flat roof and a good view —"

Startled, for Edna had never before singled him out for more than a smile, he blurted, "I guess I could — I don't care where I watch it from."

Afterward he kicked himself all the way home. He could think of a dozen gracious, polite ways to accept her invitation, but it was too late. Evidently Edna was not offended, for she said, "Come over at seven. The eclipse starts at seven-thirty."

Barney was in heaven. He was going to watch the eclipse with the prettiest girl in the class, in the school, maybe in all Philadelphia.

That night at supper he was vague about just where he was going to station himself to watch the

75

big event. Pop had decreed that even Isaac and Rob could stay up to watch it, for it would not happen again for a long time. Benjie and Morris were going to the intersection of Tenth and Reed where they could get a broad view of the sky. Ida and Adella were going to watch from the O'Riley house, because the house across the street from theirs was only two stories high, and the view would be clearer, they thought. Mom said that for once she was glad they had no tree in front of their house, and she and Pop and the little ones would be able to see perfectly well from their own front steps. In the discussion no one noticed that Barney hadn't said a word.

Right after supper he sneaked upstairs and washed thoroughly, at least all the parts that could be seen, and put on a clean shirt. He pulled up his stockings so they did not wrinkle over the tops of his shoes and slicked down his hair as best he could. His wiry curls sprung right up again, but he had tried. There was so much commotion that no one noticed his going.

The Carrolls lived five blocks away. He tried to time it so he rang the bell at exactly seven. Edna's Aunt Josephine answered. She had never married and lived with her brother and his family and gave music lessons.

"Do come in," she said. "You must be Ida and Adella's little brother. Such lovely girls. Edna, your

76

gentleman caller is here." Barney turned crimson. He had never thought of himself as anyone's gentleman caller. He stumbled after Miss Carroll into the front parlor and was greeted pleasantly by Mr. and Mrs. Carroll and Edna and several neighbors whose names he did not catch. Willie was nowhere to be seen. He probably was at Tenth and Reed with the rest of the gang.

They were going to have dessert while they waited, and Mrs. Carroll brought out a beautiful cake on a high glass stand. It looked too pretty to cut, for she had iced it with the picture of a smiling moon face. There was also a chocolate cake for those who preferred it, and hot chocolate. At Barney's house they called it cocoa and they drank it out of the same cups that served for tea or coffee. But at Edna's house they had a special chocolate set, a pot taller and thinner than a teapot, with a long curved spout, and tall narrow cups. It was all set out on a tea cloth so heavily embroidered with flowers that the saucers rocked slightly. It was overwhelmingly fancy, but not so overwhelming that Barney lost his appetite. Under Mrs. Carroll's kind urging he first had two slices of the moon cake and then a generous slab of the chocolate cake with several cups of hot chocolate to wash it down.

He and Edna sat side by side on an uncomfortable little horsehair sofa. The black horsehair was slippery and he kept his toes pressed firmly against the flowered carpet to keep from sliding off. The horsehair was prickly, too. He could feel it right through his stockings. The urge to scratch was almost unbearable, but he concentrated on eating in an effort to forget it. He was determined not to disgrace himself by scratching.

There was no need for either of them to say anything. The grownups did all the talking. Mr. Carroll explained in great detail about the eclipse. It would have been quite instructive if Miss McGowen hadn't been through it all that very afternoon. But the ladies were very interested.

Then one of the neighbors asked if Miss Josephine would favor them with a selection on the piano while they waited. Miss Josephine went to the piano in the back parlor to play what she called a little moon music. First there was something pretty called "The Moon on the Cherry Blossoms." Barney wished Ida would learn that. It would be a nice change. Then she played "Clair de Lune," which she explained was French for "the light of the moon." Then a long song — for Edna's aunt sang as well — called "When the Corn Is Waving, Annie, Dear" in which the moon was at the full, and then "The Rose of Tralee" where the pale moon was rising above the green mountain. It was all very nice, and helpful, too, for Barney had eaten so much that his stomach was making odd noises. Nobody noticed with all the music.

The recital went on and on. Barney's toes had gone to sleep, but he dared not wiggle them for fear of falling off the sofa. Slowly, carefully, he slid sideways so that one foot could be firmly planted on the floor while he tried to stir some life into the other. Just when he thought he could stand it no longer, the parlor clock chimed.

Mrs. Carroll cried out, "We've missed it! We've missed the eclipse!"

There was no point in going to the roof. A glance out the parlor window showed that the moon was full and bright again. The eclipse was over.

They all said goodnight, and the neighbors assured the Carrolls that the delicious refreshments and delightful music were much more interesting than any old eclipse. Barney said only "Thank you for a lovely evening" and made his way home as fast as he could.

Everyone was still talking about the momentous occasion. Barney agreed when Mom asked, "Wasn't it scary when the moon went really dark?" And Pop said, "Well, it wasn't completely black, sort of deep blood red —" He agreed to whatever anyone said, but he offered no observations of his own.

It was a bitter disappointment. He had missed a world-shaking event, tomorrow Miss McGowen would expect them all to write a composition about it, and on top of that he was uncomfortably full. He belched from time to time as he tried to get to sleep. "Girls!" he thought.

He had decided to have no more to do with girls, ever, when a few days later the Soupy Island invitation came. Now here was an event, and surely nothing could go wrong! Besides, the invitation came from Willie Carroll, not Edna.

The Soupy Island trip was an annual Presbyterian outing, but each Presbyterian family was allowed a guest, and the Carrolls had chosen Barney.

Two sisters, Miss Elizabeth and Miss Lucy Monroe, were the two wealthy benefactors who each year sponsored a boat trip to an island in the Delaware River. What the island's real name was Barney never knew. It was just known as Soupy Island, where the sisters dispensed hot soup and other picnic food. It was an exclusive picnic. Barney was the only Reed Streeter invited.

All dressed up in the white sailor suit that had been Benjie's, Barney looked fine. The suit had been bleached and pressed until it looked like new, and there was a whistle on a cord that fitted in the breast pocket. He carried his bathing suit and his towel and went to meet the Carrolls. They walked in a sedate group to the church where the special horse-drawn buses were waiting. Lots of them, for there were a lot of Presbyterians. He sat between Willie and Edna and scuffled his feet in the straw that covered the floor. None of the Presbyterians would spit on the floor, of course, but the straw was there anyway.

At the dock they all crowded on a boat called officially the *Elizabeth Monroe*, but known as the "Miss Lizzie." Somewhere he had heard that there was also a boat called the *Lucy Monroe*. Perhaps their father was a shipbuilder. Anyway, they certainly were generous ladies.

It was a fascinating trip. There were plenty of seats, but it was more fun to stand. Barney hung over the rail and watched the trash in the river churn past. Soon Edna tugged at his middy blouse and said, "Be careful, Barnett, you'll fall over." He backed away reluctantly. It was a little like going on a trip with your mother.

It was lunch time when they docked at Soupy Island. It didn't look like much — a sandy little beach, some scraggly trees with a lot of picnic tables set out, two big wooden bathhouses for changing, and a playground with swings and other amusements. As soon as they landed they sang a few Presbyterian hymns, which Barney didn't know, and then they all lined up for lunch.

As they passed by the long serving tables they were given a choice of sandwiches and a big tin cup.

Then Miss Lizzie and Miss Lucy filled each cup with a dipper of hot soup from a steaming kettle. They could go back as often as they liked, and Willie did. Barney was making a terrific effort to be worthy of the occasion, so he went back only once. Then there were cookies, one apiece, and a glass of lemonade.

Miss Lizzie announced that no swimming would be allowed for a full hour, at which time a bell would ring. In the meantime, the elders would sing and hear speeches, and the children could play.

The sun was hot and Barney felt too full to be happy about pushing the round-about and then jumping on for a short spin. He would have preferred to swing, but Edna said that the round-about was her favorite, so he pushed and ran and pushed and ran while Edna rode round and round.

It was a relief when the bell rang and they could go into the bathhouse and change for swimming. Outside again, Barney looked around for Willie, but Edna was waiting.

"I can't swim," she said. "I'm counting on you to look after me, Barnett." She looked at him with her melting blue eyes.

"I'll teach you," he offered.

"I don't want to get my hair wet. We'll just splash here in the shallow water," she decided.

Out in the deeper water, Willie and a bunch of other boys were swimming with what sounded like wild enthusiasm. Barney listened wistfully while he splashed in the shallow water with Edna and dozens of toddlers and their mothers. It was not his idea of a swimming party.

After an endless time, the bell rang again and everyone was called out of the water to get dressed for the trip home. This time he made no effort to comb his hair. His curls could fly all over the place for all he cared.

They gathered for one last hymn and a speech of thanks to the Monroe sisters. Then back on the "Lizzie Monroe" and home in the late afternoon.

Reed Street had never looked so good. Mom had fixed an especially nice supper.

"No appetite, I'll bet, Barney, after all that lovely picnic. You should take a bite, even so."

He ate as if he had never eaten before. Benjie asked, "Well, what about it? How was the picnic?"

"Swell," he answered, trying to sound sincere.

"You lucky dog," said Morris.

A dog would have had more fun, thought Barney. A dog would have been out there swimming.

He thought about it that night before he went to sleep.

"Girls are only trouble," he decided. "From now

on I'm going to steer clear of 'em, hair ribbons or not. I'm never going to get mixed up with a girl again. Except maybe once in a while —''

He fell asleep before he could decide how he would choose the girls to get mixed up with.

9

School was out at last! The whole wonderful summer
lay ahead of Barney, full of nothing but joys. When
he stopped to think about it, there were daily chores,
of course, and errands to run. But with good man-
gement, and Barney was a very good manager when
it came to chores, most of his time would be free. If
he worked it right, Rob would be learning to take
over some of his jobs, and would feel very grown-up
and proud doing them.

Pop decided that this was the year the cellar walls
must be whitewashed, two coats, but that was a job

Benjie and Morris and Barney shared. It took only two mornings of rather pleasant splashing around in the thick whitewash, dressed in their oldest clothes. Then Barney and Willie Carroll helped Charley whitewash the Schermerdine cellar. Otherwise Charley would have been at it all summer and never would have a minute to play. It was hard to please Mrs. Schermerdine, but they did it. When it was over there was the fun of sluicing off under the pump in the back yard.

Their small earth plot had been turned over early in the spring. Each morning all the boys put in a few minutes weeding between the rows of cosmos and sweet william and zinnias, edged neatly with parsley. Mom's Heaven Blue morning glories grew on the trellis over the unused outhouse, a miracle as they slowly uncurled from long pointed buds to partly opened buds and then purple-throated beauty. Vegetables were cheap from the huckster, and there was no need to try to grow them in their small space.

The ashes had to be taken out each morning, but they had worked out a fair schedule for this, and it took only a few minutes. Once a week the kitchen stove had to be blacked and the nickel trim polished, but that chore was often used as punishment for whichever boy had misbehaved — or rather, had been caught. No problem. They were used to all this.

The two girls had a different set of chores. They helped Mom with the housework and the cooking. They went shopping with Mom to learn how things were done. They watched as she chose the live chickens. She showed them how to hold the flapping bird firmly by the feet and blow in its soft feathered behind. If the skin there showed fat and firm and yellow, it was a chicken worth stewing. There were a lot of things to learn about housekeeping, and Mom was determined that her daughters would be well trained.

The boys were required to keep their own rooms neat. If their standards were never quite up to Mom's, it created only a small fuss. Then there was a trip to the corner store if Mom was especially busy, an errand for old Miss Ferguson, and afterward the whole day was waiting for them.

They could go down to the river at Delaware and Reed and hang around the freight cars that brought the blackstrap molasses to the sugar refineries. No matter how carefully it was piped off, sometimes the gooey molasses seeped out around the couplings. There it was, just begging to be scooped off and eaten, right out of the hand. Right out of some pretty grubby hands. Once in a while, as he licked the last drops from his fingers, Barney thought of what Mom would say, then hastily switched his thoughts to something else. The dirt never seemed to hurt any of them — they thrived on it.

They could play ball in Kolb's lot, or fight when necessary. There were a number of swell things to do, but "going down the Neck" was considered the swellest. The gang drifted together at Kleinhoffer's corner. They would wait awhile for any latecomers, and then when it was clear that all who could come were there, they started off.

The Neck was a piece of land way down Broad Street. Acres of marshes and burning dumps and little creeks that ran out to the Delaware River. There was fertile flat land, too, cultivated by farmers known as Neckers, whose truck gardens supplied the vegetables that the hucksters brought to Reed Street.

It was a long hot trudge across Passayunk to Broad Street and then down Broad, three miles or more, to where the houses were farther and farther apart and then where there were no houses at all. It was hard on the bare feet not yet really toughened for the summer. But it was worth it.

Their pond was a nameless puddle, thick and dark brown, more mud than water. But they passed up others, some with cleaner water, because the struggle to get through the sharp marsh grass was too hard.

Every boy on Reed Street had learned to swim in this pond, and in a year or so it would be Rob's turn. If Mom had known what the water was like she would have fainted first and then forbidden the whole wonderful trek. It would have been impossible to explain its charm to her — the bright hot sky overhead like a great blue bowl, the smell of salty marsh grass and brackish water, the real stink of the burning dumps that smoked constantly, the cries of startled red-winged blackbirds, all melted into a heady mixture, sound and sight and smell.

Mom wouldn't have understood it. She would have let out a screech at the sight of the muddy pond, full of goodness only knows what, and that would have been the end of it. Just as well she didn't know. Mrs. Vitalli would have felt the same way, and Mrs. O'Riley, and certainly Mrs. Schermerdine!

About three miles down Broad Street they turned off toward the river. There was a wooden bridge over the freight tracks, and after that was crossed, a winding path through the mushy marsh to the pond. Their pond was perfect because the tall grass did not grow to the very edge of it. There was a rim of short grass and earth where they could strip off their clothes and change into swimming trunks, baggy cotton knit pants held up by a drawstring that each one tightened around his skinny waist. If the pants slipped off in the muddy water they would be lost forever. Barney often wondered why they had to bother with swimming trunks at all. There was no one to see them. But mothers expected them to start off with dry trunks and come home with wet ones. It was the custom.

The cold water felt great on their perspiring bodies. "Last one in is a Chinaman" or an Eskimo or a Hottentot — but they hit the water almost at the same time. They splashed and squealed and held their noses as they dived to the bottom to fumble in the mud for rocks. More often they brought up old tin cans or bottles. None of them, even the big boys, swam with any style, just a slight improvement on the primitive dog paddle. The pond was hardly more than four feet deep, but it felt deeper and dangerous because of the thick muddy bottom.

They came out when the sun stood straight overhead, pulling off the leeches that clung to them. Barney hated them. He hated to touch the leeches, to have to grasp them and pull them off almost turned his stomach. But he never said a word. He just tore the awful sucking things from his skin with his teeth clenched and threw them in the grass behind him. If he had admitted his weakness, Lumpy and Joe and Willie would have laughed and put their leeches on him. He could see that Charley dreaded them too, but much as he wanted to, he couldn't help his friend. Charley would have to get toughened to leeches just as he had, or pretend to. He wondered sometimes if Benjie and the others felt the same. Or were they really as brave as they seemed? It was hard to tell. The nearer people got to being grown-up, the harder it was to tell.

They ate their lunches on the bank of the pond, sharing an interesting variety. On a Friday, the Vitallis and the O'Rileys and the Finnerans all had cheese or egg sandwiches, and could not switch, but on other days it could be salami or pastrami or a nice cold knockwurst sliced on rye or pickles and meat loaf. And several bottles of soda pop apiece, for the water certainly wasn't fit to drink.

After they were comfortably stuffed they lay back on the wiry grass with their arms folded under their heads. They talked lazily about a lot of things — of what they planned to do with the rest of the summer, mostly, but other things too. Like when Barney said to Lumpy, "When your mom sees the color of that string on your medals, won't she guess this water is pretty dirty?"

"We wash 'em under the pump. I keep a piece of soap out there just to wash the string."

"Mine is on a chain," said Francis Finneran proudly. "We all got chains for our St. Christophers."

"Papa gets steady work, we'll have chains, too."

They all nodded. They could all understand how it was, even the ones who didn't wear medals.

Later they swam again, when they decided an hour had passed. Maybe it was a short hour. Anyway, before long they were back in again, yelling and splashing.

When at last the sun was beginning to slant low over toward Broad Street, they got out and dressed. The walk down was long, but then the fun was ahead of them and they didn't mind. Going back always seemed longer. The sidewalks had had all day to soak up the heat and by late afternoon they were sizzling. So they dried off and dressed reluctantly, hating to leave, dreading the time when they would leave the grassy path and go over the bridge to Broad Street.

They lingered at the bridge. There was always the chance that a freight train would pass just as they were going over, with the engine puffing steam and cinders and the sparks flying from the smoke stack. If they hung over the rail and yelled and waved, the engineer would wave back and toot the whistle. This day, there was no train in sight, so they trudged across, not saying much, until Charley yelled, "Ouch!"

"Splinters," said Benjie. "Have to watch out for them."

"No," insisted Charley, "I'm burnt!"

They might not have paid much attention to his complaint except that Joe started to yell, too.

"Fire!" he screamed. "My foot's on fire! The bridge is on fire! Call the engines!"

A quick look showed that Charley and Joe were right. The sparks from a train that roared past maybe hours ago had lodged in a crack in the bridge, and one of the planks was smoldering. There was no flame, but if a breeze came up and fanned it, before long the whole bridge would be on fire. The dry wood would burn like kindling.

It was a long run to the nearest house on Broad Street, a mile, at least.

Lumpy said, "We'll bring water from the pond —" and then remembered that they had nothing to carry it in. Their lunches had been wrapped in newspaper, their towel bags were cloth.

There might have been men who could help, way over by the dumps, but none of them, not even Benjie or Joe, was brave enough to venture over there. The derelicts who lived in discarded packing crates and sorted through the trash and garbage were a wild, outcast bunch. Nothing, not even the burning bridge, would have made one of the boys go in that direction. They had to solve this one themselves.

"Tin cans," said Benjie, taking charge. "We'll go

back and collect enough tin cans and keep bringing them full of water. You stay here, Barney, and watch that it doesn't get any bigger.''

Barney wanted to run with the others to the pond, but Benjie was in charge, so he obeyed. He watched the little hot spot anxiously. It was not a big fire but it certainly could make trouble. He wished the others would hurry. They were hurrying, of course, but the pond was some distance away. He could see them running toward it, winding through the tall grass. Then he looked at the fire again, still no bigger, thank goodness.

He thought about supper. They'd be late, but with an excuse like this, Mom wouldn't scold. He was ready for supper right now. Lunch was a long time ago and he was hungry. Hungry — and something else. He should have gone before he left the pond — and all of a sudden the answer came to him. He, Barney, could put the fire out all by himself. He was grateful for the three bottles of orange crush he had polished off for lunch.

It only took a moment. The hot board sizzled as the thin stream hit it. Barney sprayed all around until the board was thoroughly soaked. He had squeezed out the last few drops and buttoned up his pants again by the time the rest of the gang came racing up carrying assorted cans and bottles of water.

"The fire's under control," he said modestly. "I peed it out."

They dumped their cans of water anyway, but Barney was right. The fire was out and he was the one who had taken care of it.

Barney was the big hero all the way home. Even Benjie and Joe and Lumpy patted him on the back. Somehow the hot sidewalks seemed not so hot as they talked about how smart the kid was — young but smart. Barney thought about being a fireman someday. He certainly showed talent in that direction. Mostly he thought about how good Mom's supper would taste.

It was all very well to be a hero on the way home, but it didn't last long. At the table, after the first busy chewing was over and conversation began, Pop asked, "So? How did the swimming go?"

Benjie, as the oldest boy, started to tell the story, with all praise going to Barney. But as he reached the crucial point, Mom realized what was going to come.

"Ida! Adella! Leave the table. This is not for young ladies."

Ida and Adella obeyed, of course, but lingered in the kitchen within hearing.

"Now, Barnett, I'm not saying you shouldn't have. In an emergency, well — but not to brag about! You saved maybe hundreds of dollars for the railroad. That's good. Just don't spread it around the neighborhood how it happened, that's all I ask. If Dora hears about it —''

"Esther," protested Pop. "Barney deserves credit. Credit he should get. A problem came up, he thought of an answer fast, he used his head."

"Jacob," said Mom, "it wasn't his head he used."

Pop said solemnly, "My good and loving Esther, I see what you mean." But his lips twitched as if he wanted very much to laugh.

10

There was no stable on Barney's block of Reed Street. No one there was in the ice or produce or hauling business. Certainly no one in that neighborhood owned their own carriage horse. But in addition to the big Kolb stables just behind Reed Street, South Philadelphia was dotted with them, large and small.

You knew when you were coming to one of them, in the summer especially, from the smell. Not an unpleasant smell, but distinctively stable. A good horsey smell mixed with the fragrance of baled straw and hay in the loft overhead.

Any stable had a fascination for Barney. He found if he hung around long enough, finally some hostler would permit him to lead the horse back and forth, back and forth, while a system of pulleys attached to the cathead on the stable roof hauled the bales of hay into the loft. Often he and Charley were trusted to go up in the loft, break open a bale of straw and pitch it down through the trap door to the stalls below. The stable hands enjoyed the chance to lie back in the hay and rest while they ordered the sweating boys around.

Nothing made Mom madder than when Barney came home all covered with bits of hay and straw. "Shake off your clothes before you track all that mess through my clean house! And wash your feet under the pump. And then tell me why you boys will do anything to get out of work at home, and then for nothing go off to work for somebody else. Tell me, does Hogan's delivery man cook for you? Does he bake you a pie in this hot weather? Does he give you a penny, even? Not so much as a penny!"

Barney had no answer. Work around the house had no charm at all, while work at a stable was a delight.

Some of the lofts were only half filled with hay, and the rest partitioned off into a nice big room for a club house. There would be a table for pinochle or poker, an ice chest for the beer and a few interesting magazines with pictures of ladies in very low-cut dresses.

Pop didn't belong to a club like this. "I should work all day for a dollar and maybe lose it in ten minutes of pinochle with a bunch of roughnecks?" When Pop played pinochle it was with his brother-in-law Joseph, Aunt Bessie's husband, who laughed a lot, and with Mom's brother Martin who never laughed at all because he was married to Aunt Dora. At least that's the way it seemed to Barney.

Pop belonged to the Ethical and Benefit Society. He was usually elected the president because he was good at figuring. Every week each member put in a small amount, and at the end of the year the interest it gathered in the bank was divided. When Pop brought home the receipts at night he put the money in a bag and then rolled it carelessly in a piece of newspaper. He strolled along as if he was carrying nothing more valuable than a two-cent dried herring. Pop was not a big man, but he was strong, and if anyone had tried to take away that package he would have fought like a tiger.

At the end of each year the members commissioned Mr. S. D. Holt, Aristocratic Penmanship, to make a diploma. Pop's photograph would be at the top, then pictures of the four or five directors, and then the list of members beautifully handwritten by Mr. Holt himself. They all marveled at the flowing letters. It was hard to believe that a human hand could guide a pen in such scrolls and twirls. It was something to be proud of, to be a member of the Ethical and Benefit Society, yet the hayloft clubs had a different kind of appeal.

It was because of a hayloft club that Barney got involved for the last time with Smelly Huggins. He should have known better. He did know better, but the lure of the loft club was too strong.

It started when Rob came home in tears one afternoon. Rob's friends had marked out a ring in the hard-packed earth on Kolb's lot and were busy playing marbles. Smelly, always alert for a good deal, kindly offered to give the youngsters some pointers, and in a few minutes had won all the marbles the six-year-olds owned, all of them.

It was clear that someone had to do something. Adella wanted to go straight to Mrs. Huggins and demand justice, but Rob begged her not to. At the moment Barney was the only Freedman boy home. "I'll handle this," he said, boiling with indignation. He caught Smelly at the end of the alley, smiling to himself, carrying his big bag of marbles.

Pop always said, "Violence is the last resort of a coward. Always try to reason first." So Barney decided to try it the way Pop would approve.

"Come on, we're going to play for those marbles.

And you know I can win 'em back, so let's get started."

"No," whined Smelly. "I won them. I get to keep them. I won't play you."

"Give 'em back, then. Those little kids are just learning to play. You knew you'd win. You're a low-down cheat!"

"Not on your life. They're mine now."

It was clear that reason had lost. Barney was so mad that he forgot Smelly was pounds heavier, two inches taller and immeasurably meaner.

"Give the marbles back or I'll punch you, and when Benjie comes home he'll mess you up so you'll wish —"

"Now, wait," said Smelly. "Don't bring Benjie into this. Let's discuss it, man to man."

"Man to monkey, and you know which is which. There's nothing to discuss. You cheated the little kids, and cheaters get punched."

Barney had his dukes up, ready to go. Smelly quickly reconsidered. "I could give back some if your brother is such a sore loser."

"All," said Barney, "and that means yours, too, or I'll get Lumpy and Joe to help Benjie."

Smelly gave in quickly, if not happily. He handed over the bag and then asked, "No hard feelings?"

"No good feelings, either, you low-down snake.

And remember, you try something like this again and we'll *all* be laying for you — Benjie and Morris and Joe and Lumpy and Francis and Willie —"

"Don't tell them. Don't tell them anything and I'll show you something special."

"Anything you got to show I wouldn't want to see."

"How about a look at the Jolly Fellows Social Club in Harrison's loft? It's all fixed up for a party tonight. My father belongs, so I can sneak you in."

Barney was torn. He wanted to tell Smelly what to do with his old Jolly Fellows Social Club, and yet he wanted so much to see the inside. It was the best known and rowdiest of all the loft clubs and the most exclusive. Finally he gave in.

"Okay, I won't tell Benjie and the others — but only if you let the little kids alone."

Smelly now seemed anxious to be friends.

"Close your eyes while I get the key," he said, when they arrived at Harrison's stable. "I wouldn't dare let anyone know where it's kept. They'd kill me."

Barney closed his eyes tight while Smelly fumbled around somewhere and then opened them again to follow Smelly up the steep ladder. Smelly explained as he led the way, "The party tonight's for the initiation. It's really going to be something."

Barney hated to have to ask "What's an initiation?" but he wanted to know.

"It's when they take in a new member, stupid. They make him go through a lot of tests to prove he's worthy. They wouldn't let your pop in even if he passed the tests, because he's a Jew."

"That's fair enough," said Barney, too busy looking to take offense. "They wouldn't let any of your family in the synagogue. They'd stink up the place. You'd all have to be fumigated first."

The clubhouse was indeed fancy. It was festooned with colored streamers draped from the ceiling to the lamp hanging over the big card table. On the walls were posters of smiling ladies with almost no clothes on at all. Barney looked away quickly to the icebox. Smelly opened it to show how it was stocked with ice and cheese and rye bread and room for many quart buckets of beer.

Smelly displayed a machine in the corner. "You hit this with the sledge hammer, see, and you can see how many pounds of strength you got by how high the marker goes. They only take in strong guys. Then they turn out the lights and lead the new guy around, and drop paper bags of water on him, here — close your eyes and I'll show you —"

Barney obeyed. He stumbled after Smelly and stepped on something sharp that hurt his bare foot, and something else flew up and hit him on the forehead so hard he saw stars. He was dazed by the blow, and it took him an instant to realize what had happened. He had stepped on a carefully concealed hoe and the handle had flown up and hit him. Smelly was doubled up with laughter.

"You think you're so smart," he chortled. "You've got the marbles, but you've got the bump, too."

At the same time Barney felt the lump rising on his forehead, he felt his anger rising inside. This time Smelly had gone too far. Boiling with rage, he grabbed the hoe and started after his longtime enemy. Smelly took one look at him and began to back away.

"Now wait — look here — can't you take a little joke? Don't you dare hit me —"

As Smelly backed away, Barney advanced on him with the hoe raised. Smelly backed faster, out of the club room and through the door into the hay storage room.

"Wait, wait — I'll tell my pop — don't you dare —"

There was a sudden thump as Smelly disappeared from sight. He had backed right through the open trap door and down into the stall below. Without a second thought Barney dropped the hoe and jumped on top of him. He knew that he had hit Smelly with terrific force, mashing him absolutely flat. It was lucky that there was a fair padding of straw underneath. Smelly's nose gushed blood.

"I give up," he blubbered. "Uncle, uncle," though strictly speaking it was not a fight at all.

"Repeat after me," said Barney through clenched teeth. "Say it or I won't let you up. Say 'as long as I live I will never set foot on Ninth and Reed Street again, so help me God!' Say it!"

"I can't — I have to go to school that way."

"Then go around. Say it!"

Really crying now, Smelly repeated the solemn oath.

"And say, 'I'll never again lay a hand on any Reed Streeter or try to cheat any of them.' Say it!"

Smelly said it, and Barney got up and left the stable without a backward glance. He looked awful. The lump on his head felt as big as an egg, and it throbbed painfully. His blouse was stained all over from Smelly's nosebleed. His pants were torn where they had caught on a rough board as he jumped through the trap door.

He opened the alley gate cautiously, hoping that he could get upstairs before Mom saw him. She was taking down the clothes. As the gate creaked, she turned around and let out a screech.

"Barney! What happened?"

When he tried to explain, and she got over being frightened, she got mad. "So now you're a brawling street fighter! My son Barnett, good only for fights! Come on, get some ice on that lump. And your pants — take off that blouse — where are you bleeding from?''

"It's Smelly Huggins' blood," he said. "And I'm not sorry. I don't care if he doesn't have any blood left.''

"My son, the fighter! I'm supposed to be proud? I'm supposed to run around maybe and tell all the neighbors how my fine son can make another boy bleed and ruin a good white blouse? You expect me to be happy now? Your pop will have something to say about this!''

Barney didn't care. At long last, Smelly had got his comeuppance, and he, Barnett Freedman, had given it to him.

But one thing he found out for sure. He did not want to grow up to be a prize fighter. He didn't really like fighting, although the scrimmage with Smelly had been more an accident than a fight. But even if he did, even if he became Champion of the World, he knew he couldn't handle his mother.

11

The Fourth of July started early. The Freedman boys were all up almost as soon as it was light, but even before that, someone set off the first firecracker in the alley. It was a loud one and jolted them all out of their sleep. Mom and Pop groaned. It was a holiday, and they looked forward to a few minutes of extra sleep before the excitement of the big day began in earnest. But it was no use. Another firecracker — it must have been a whopper — boomed right after the first one and Mom and the girls staggered sleepily out of bed to start breakfast.

"No one leaves this house without a good break-fast," Mom ordered groggily. "Everybody eats, or you don't go out at all." The boys knew she didn't really mean it. Nothing short of a catastrophe would keep them in on the Fourth of July, but they were hungry anyway, and the family picnic would not come until much later in the day.

So they shoveled down their oatmeal and toast and made their beds, complaining loudly that they would be the last ones out on Reed Street.

"So good," said Mom. "The later the noise starts, the better I like it. Watch Rob, Morris. He's not to shoot off any big ones. Isaac stays right here with Ida and Adella."

Isaac set up a howl, was whacked on his sturdy little bottom and settled down with Ida and Adella and the O'Riley girls and the youngest Vitalli boys and girls with their supply of spit devils and snakes.

Barney went through his bag of treasures and tried to figure how he could get the most noise and excitement out of the firecrackers he had managed to save for. There were strings of little Chinese firecrackers in red and gold paper to light and throw, some to catch in tree branches if possible, others to be thrown out in the street. Once in a while a cellar door was left propped open, and a firecracker thrown down there echoed delightfully. The little ones went off in a string of fast pops, but there were larger ones that made a real roar, magnified by the tin can that you placed over the cracker. When one of those went off, the whole block shook, the tin can flew roof high and fell with a clatter that added to the noise.

Barney had not invested heavily in spit devils, much as he enjoyed them. He began his day by spinning on his heel and crushing one, then went spitting and crackling down the street with the bits of gunpowder stuck in the heels of his shoes, exploding as he went.

Shoes were a requirement. For spit devils, and to be properly dressed for the parade and speeches in the park later on. He hoarded the rest of his spit devils to crush on the sidewalk at the park. Ladies in long dresses and flowered hats leaped and squealed when they stepped on them. The more they scraped to get the spit devil fragments off their shoes, the more explosions they got. It added zest to the political speeches and zing to the band music.

If he was lucky he could pick up enough money for a few more firecrackers before the day was over. A string of firecrackers thrown under an already nervous horse could cause quite a lot of rearing and lunging. Then a boy who was fast on his feet could leap for the bridle, calm the excited animal and get a generous tip from the frightened driver. It was hard on the horse, Barney thought, but the possibility for ready cash was right there, and if his conscience reared and lunged a little, too, he calmed it by saying that no one with a lick of sense should be out driving on the Fourth.

Then he hurried to the drugstore to spend his money on another string of firecrackers and maybe a torpedo or two. The drugstore always stayed open even though it was a holiday. People ran out of firecrackers, and they also ran out of bandages and iodine. There were a lot of cuts and burns to be taken care of. Sometimes even serious wounds.

The din was awful, and very satisfying to a boy's heart. The grownups might complain all day, but the children loved it, danger and all.

Lunch was catch-as-catch-can. Mom made a platter of sandwiches and a huge pitcher of lemonade and left them on the kitchen table. As they got hungry, they ran home, snatched enough to keep them going, and dashed out again. Barney also had a quick lunch at Charley's house and enjoyed a salami sandwich with Lumpy and Joe.

Mrs. Vitalli yelled as the boys dashed in and out, "The screen door slams once more, I'll slam you all! Keep clean for the speeches!" It was just like being at home.

Charley was ordered home to change his clothes again for the celebration in the park. Mrs. Schermerdine was very nervous, and the sight of Charley even slightly mussed got her upset. He made a quick job of it, though, and joined the others at one o'clock sharp.

It was not much of a park — a triangle of grass and hard-packed earth where three streets ran together. There were enough buttonwood trees for some shade, and the smart ones got there in time to sit on the folding chairs supplied free by the Dagney Funeral Parlor. There was a brand new paper fan advertising the business on each chair. They were needed today, for it was a hot one, and even hotter if you came late and had to stand in the sun. A bandstand had been built in the center with a podium for the speakers.

Barney and the other boys avoided their families as if a plague had broken out. Mom would signal for them to come and sit down with the family and behave properly and keep clean, and none of them intended to do any of that. They swarmed up the trees and made themselves as comfortable as possible on the hard branches to wait for the parade to begin.

"They're late," said Willie.

"They always begin late," answered Barney. He squirmed around to find a back rest against the trunk of the tree. "No parade ever starts on time."

There was quite a wait, and a lot of calling from anxious mothers about being careful, not falling, no whistling while the speeches were going on, and so

111

on. They ignored it all happily, knowing they'd catch it later and not caring. It was the Fourth of July, and who cared about obeying on the Fourth of July?

At last the first strident notes of the band were heard, and the American flag was borne up the street, held by the head of the Patriots' Association. The band was playing "The Stars and Stripes Forever." Even up in the tree, Barney's feet moved to the marching beat. Many of the musicians were the same ones who played outside Kleinhoffer's Saloon, old friends. Then came the Veterans of the Spanish American War and next the old fellows from the Civil War. Then a dozen or so automobiles chugged by, wildly decorated with flags and bunting.

"There's a Hupmobile!" shouted Morris.

"And there's a Spitz! And a Velie —"

No one Barney knew owned an automobile, but there were plenty of them around, noisy, kicking up clouds of dust, scaring horses and ladies. Barney knew he wouldn't be afraid to ride in one, but his chances seemed pretty slim.

Then the Social groups came by. The Free Enterprisers, the Tuesday and Fridays and finally the Jolly Fellows, the largest and grandest of all. They wore uniforms of sorts, straw hats trimmed with wide bands of red, white, and blue ribbon, and tricolored sashes across their chests that proclaimed "Liberty and Justice to All."

Barney looked at Smelly Huggins. He was grinning and waving from his seat up front, and yelling, "Hey, Pop! That's Pop's club!" He never looked toward the tree the Freedman boys and their friends had staked out.

Mom had declared that Rob was not to climb the tree, that he must sit beside her and Pop and the girls, but even though he had not been allowed to climb the tree, he and Isaac had managed to escape and were running now alongside the Jolly Fellows Club, cheering.

Barney thought grimly, "Those little traitors, I'll get them!" But then the festive excitement of the day softened him. They were just young, that was all. Later he could take them aside and explain nicely that under no circumstances whatever were they to cheer the Jolly Fellows Club, or he would skin the hides off his younger brothers.

When the parade had straggled around the park three times — it was not a big parade so they stretched it out as long as possible — and the band had mounted the stand, Father Flanagan from the Church of the Annunciation climbed the steps to the podium. There was a certain amount of muttering from the crowd, for it had been originally planned that Pastor Hoffman from the Lutheran church would open the ceremonies. Somehow they had worked it out so Pastor Hoffman would deliver the

113

benediction. That was not as good a spot, for by that time people were beginning to drift away toward the picnics that waited at home. Anyway, that was what was printed on the program, so both sides settled down to listen. The band played a few patriotic numbers. Up in the tree, the boys could not stand at attention but they held their caps across their hearts and saluted the flag as "The Star-Spangled Banner" was played.

Then Congressman O'Donnell was introduced and he began his speech. His voice roared out over the crowd, on and on and on. He gave the whole glorious history of the country from the first brave Pilgrims up to the very day of July 4, 1911.

The branches grew harder as the speech went on. Barney shifted one way and then the other. "My bottom's gone to sleep," he whispered to Morris. Charley giggled at that and made Willie laugh. Then Barney's feet began to tingle. He wiggled his ankles, but the pins-and-needles feeling was almost unbearable. He tried to keep his mind off his uncomfortable seat, and cautiously stood up, leaning back against the tree trunk. It was warm, even up among the leaves of the tree. He began to fan vigorously with his program and that gave him an idea. He folded the program carefully and sent it flying down toward the front row where Smelly Huggins sat. It missed, and sailed low over the podium.

Congressman O'Donnell hesitated for an instant as the program shot over his head, but only for an instant. He was too far gone in his speech to falter now.

Benjie quickly folded his, too, and Lumpy and Joe followed. One after another the programs swooped down. Every head in the audience turned toward the trees, shocked at this irreverence.

Isaac pointed and shouted proudly, "That's Barney!"

Barney shrank back against the tree trunk to hide behind a leafy branch. If his feet hadn't been asleep, he might have managed better. As it was, he scrambled for a foothold and lost. Benjie reached out to grab him and was able to get a grip on his shirttail. It was a good try, but not enough to hold him. Charley let out a high-pitched scream, and Morris yelled.

Barney grabbed at a lower branch as he passed and that broke his fall a little. Mom and Pop were on their feet now, hurrying toward the buttonwood. Barney landed with a thud. He saw stars that had nothing to do with the flag. For a moment he wasn't sure of anything. The next thing he was sure of was Mom leaning over him and Pop saying, "Don't move him! Something may be broken!"

Old Dr. Jenkins was in the front row, and he leaped up and ran over. Congressman O'Donnell was completely ignored. His speech ran down and petered out while his audience left him.

Dr. Jenkins and Mr. Hughes, the pharmacist, felt Barney all over and then gently helped him sit up. Doc Jenkins pulled down his eyelids and looked carefully at his eyeballs.

"Do you remember your name, son?" asked Doc.

Barney would rather not have said it aloud. "Barnett Freedman," he whispered.

"And where do you live?"

"Nine-two-o Reed."

Dr. Jenkins stood up. "His mind seems clear. Take him right home, Mrs. Freedman, and watch him. Don't let him go to sleep for at least eight hours, and if he gets incoherent or throws up, call me." He turned back to add, "Only very light stuff to eat, remember. No rich food."

Barney groaned and lay back on the ground. No picnic. It was the last straw.

Mom and Pop helped him up, and then Pop pointed at the tree, where the rest of the boys sat frozen with fear.

"I want all of you down out of that tree *this minute*," he said in a quietly fierce voice. Even Willie and Lumpy and Joe followed Morris and Benjie down the buttonwood.

"Is he going to die?" whispered Willie.

"He'd better not," said Mom firmly, "because as

soon as he's better he's going to get a licking he won't forget. Spoiling the Fourth of July speech!"

It was true. With his audience crowding around Barney, Congressman O'Donnell ran out of words. He ended rather lamely and nodded to Pastor Hoffman, who gave a hurried benediction to the few who were left. The band began to toot, and the men from Dagney's Funeral Parlor started to fold the chairs.

All through the lovely picnic in the back yard, Barney lay on the couch by the kitchen window. Mom and Ida and Adella went back and forth with a tureen of cold borscht and platters of fried chicken and pitchers of lemonade. Uncle Joseph and Aunt Bessie were there with little Rebecca and Sarah, and Uncle Martin and Aunt Dora. The flower beds were edged with small flags stuck in the ground. Pop and the uncles had carried the big kitchen table outside and covered it with Mom's best cloth.

"It may be a picnic," Mom said, "but that doesn't mean we have to eat like wild animals."

Barney didn't feel sick at all, and except for the lump on the back of his head he was as good as ever. Hungrier than ever. Mom fixed him a little clear chicken soup, not even with noodles.

"Light food, Dr. Jenkins said. Noodles might be too heavy. You're sure you feel all right?"

He sipped his soup forlornly and thought he could hear the crunching of crisp fried chicken even over all the laughing and talking outside. How did he get into these things? Why did calamities always happen to him? He had nothing but gloomy thoughts, even though his sisters and the aunts stopped in now and again to feel his forehead and sympathize. He could hear Aunt Dora saying, "I certainly hope the boy will recover, but my dear Esther, what a disgrace on the family! I almost died of shame. Stopping the Congressman's speech —"

It was comforting to hear Pop answer, "I don't see that as being so shameful. It was high time the Congressman ended his speech. He was beginning to get O'Donnell mixed up with Franklin and Washington and Jefferson, yet. No harm done, except to Barney's head."

The sound of firecrackers had slowed down to an occasional bang as everyone on Reed Street settled back to digest their dinners. Ladies everywhere said lazily, "Let's just clear the table and stack the dishes. Plenty of time to wash them later." Except of course for Mrs. Schermerdine. She couldn't rest if the dishes weren't washed and dried and put away immediately, even on the Fourth of July.

When it was dark and time for the fireworks, Barney pleaded to be allowed to get up. Mom said, "Well, you seem to be in your right mind, whatever that is, and you haven't thrown up. You feel dizzy? No? So, all right, you can sit out in the yard and watch the high ones. No running all over town, now —"

"Not even to Kolb's lot? If I walk slow, not even to see the lanterns?"

"No backtalk, or it'll be not even the sparklers. Wait now, I want you should keep the ice on that lump." She chopped off a piece of ice from the dwindling cake in the icebox and wrapped it in a dry towel. Then she helped him down the back steps. By now the relatives had gotten over being mad at him and were only kind and concerned. He basked in the warmth of their sympathy and watched as Pop lighted the sparklers from a stick of smoldering punk. He did this because he didn't want any child to get burned. Barney grinned as he thought of the gunpowder the children there had set off during the day. Sometimes it was a good thing grownups just didn't know.

When it came right down to it, there was nothing so pretty as a sparkler in the purple evening. In the light of the sizzling sparklers Ida and Adella and Mom were transformed, beautiful, and even Aunt Dora looked almost nice.

Morris and Benjie were off to Kolb's lot, and at the last minute Mom weakened and said, "Take Rob and Isaac, too, since they're so crazy to go, but

119

don't let go of them for a second. Stand well back, don't go too close, remember, when they light the big ones.''

Barney knew just how it would be. First the big boys, the really grown-up ones, would send up the Roman candles and the star clusters that went off with a boom and burst high above into a shower of stars. Then the pinwheels fastened along Kolb's fence would spin, round and round, scattering sparks and color and fire. Glorious.

They watched the high ones in hushed silence with a little ache inside as the last star drifted down the sky and winked out. Then there was a long wait that meant they were getting the paper lanterns ready.

These were Chinese lanterns, big ones, twice as tall as Pop. Red, yellow, pale green, each powered by a big candle. When the lighted candle had heated the air inside sufficiently, the lantern rose gently and floated off over the rooftops. Throughout South Philadelphia these beautiful globes of light were swaying gently in the evening air. It was dangerous, of course, and the firemen were always standing by. But it had always been done. It was the traditional end of the Fourth.

And then a little breeze sprang up. No more than a puff, but enough to set the big lanterns swaying.

A green lantern had swayed too far and the candle inside tipped over. All of a sudden the soft glow turned to a roaring blaze. Almost at the same time they heard the fire bell ringing from the firehouse.

Pop and the uncles got up and started to run, and the girls and the aunts followed. Mom got a grip on Barney and held him in his chair. "They'll tell us; we'll wait right here."

They could hear the pounding of the fire horses down Reed Street and across Tenth. The hook and ladder went by, and the pumper. Wherever it was, this was a fire worth watching, and he had to sit there, holding on to his ice pack. There was nothing for Barney and Mom to do but look at the glow in the sky and wonder.

"It's nice," said Mom after a little while. Her fan rustled in the darkness. "It's nice to sit here quiet for a change, maybe talk a little. We don't get much chance to talk, no, Barney?"

"There's always so much going on," he said. "It is sort of nice."

"So, talk."

There were plenty of things on his mind, but it was hard to put them into words. "Mom — Mom, I'm almost eleven," he began.

"It happens to us all," she said comfortingly.

"But I don't know what I'm going to be yet! I can't decide. When Morris was eleven, he knew, and Benjie —"

"Be? What's to be? Don't worry about it. Just go

121

along the best you can. Why don't you just be Barney?''

"Then I don't have to decide —"

"When it comes into your head, you'll know. What you are is fine for now. Just be Barney.''

He felt as if a great weight had been lifted from his shoulders. He leaned back in his chair, looked at the sky, and hummed "Over the Waves.''

Finally all the Freedmans trooped home again. Morris got there first. "Wow!" he yelled. "Barney, did you ever miss a great one! It landed on the roof of Harrison's stable!''

Mom asked anxiously, "They got the poor horses out?''

"Yep, right away. And the fire engine came so fast only the hayloft caught. Burned out the whole top floor. The club room is gone, though. The Jolly Fellows won't meet there for a long time.''

Smelly Huggins' father's club.

Justice had been done, and for once Barnett Freedman couldn't be blamed for it. It had turned out to be a wonderful day after all.